무자년의 가을 사흘

도서출판 아시아에서는 《바이링궐 에디션 한국 대표 소설》을 기획하여 한국의 우수한 문학을 주제별로 엄선해 국내외 독자들에게 소개합니다. 이 기획은 국내외 우수한 번역가들이 참여하여 원작의 품격을 최대한 살렸습니다. 문학을 통해 아시아의 정체성과 가치를 살피는 데 주력해 온 도서출판 아시아는 한국인의 삶을 넓고 깊게 이해하는 데 이 기획이 기여하기를 기대합니다.

Asia Publishers presents some of the very best modern Korean literature to readers worldwide through its new Korean literature series 〈Bilingual Edition Modern Korean Literature〉. We are proud and happy to offer it in the most authoritative translation by renowned translators of Korean literature. We hope that this series helps to build solid bridges between citizens of the world and Koreans through a rich in-depth understanding of Korea.

바이링궐 에디션 한국 대표 소설 036
Bi-lingual Edition Modern Korean Literature 036

Three Days of Autumn, 1948

서정인
무자년의 가을 사흘

Su Jung-in

ASIA
PUBLISHERS

Contents

무자년의 가을 사흘

Three Days of Autumn, 1948

무자년의 가을 사흘

"누가 교실에서 구슬 굴리냐?"

그는 그때 소학교 육학년이었다. 역사 시간에 이순신과 원균을 극적으로 대조하고 있던 이태순 선생이 교실 뒤쪽에서 구르륵 구르륵 하는 소리에 화를 냈다. 역적이 멀리 없었다. 공부시간에 하라는 공부 안 하고 뽀시락 장난하는 놈이 난신적자였다. 선생님은 홧김에 농담으로 하는 소리였지만 "원균 같은" 사람이라는 말은 지독한 욕이었다. 그들은 경상 우수사의 비열한 모함과 무능한 작전과, 그로 인한 영웅의 몰락과 수군의 괴멸

Three Days of Autumn, 1948

"Who's playing with marbles in class?"

He was in the sixth grade then. Mr. Yi Tae-sun,
who was making a dramatic comparison between
Yi Sun-sin and Won Kyun, snapped his head up at
the sound of marbles rattling in the back of the
classroom. Traitors walked among them. There
was no greater act of treason than fidgeting about
instead of studying in class. Calling someone Won
Kyun was a terrible insult, although the teacher
himself said it in jest when he was frustrated. They
were mourning the downfall of the hero and the
obliteration of his fleet. The Commander of Gyeong-

을 천추의 한으로 통탄하는 중이었다. 구르륵 구륵, 구슬 굴리는 소리는 그치지 않았다. 그것은 이상한 일이 아니었다. 그 방에는 구슬 굴리는 학생이 없었다.

　교실 문 두드리는 소리가 났다. 구슬소린지 먼 천둥소린지 잡음의 방해에서 벗어나 다시 흥을 돋구고 삼백오십 년 전으로 막 돌아갔던 역사 선생은 놀리던 두 팔들을 축 늘어뜨리고 학생들을 향해서, 할 수 없구나! 하는 표정으로 씩 웃어 보이고 문을 열었다. 옆 반 반장이었다. "너가 균이냐?" 하고 선생이 영문을 모르는 학생한테 한 팔을 쭉 뻗으면서 말했다. 반 학생들한테서 웃음이 터졌다. 선생의 극적 몸짓 때문인지 학생의 경악과 당혹 때문인지 분명치 않았다. 선생은 처음이라고 생각하고 학생들을 향해서 만족스럽게 활짝 웃어 보였고, 학생들은 나중이라고 생각하고 한층 더 웃음소리를 높였다. 그들에게는 몇 백 년 전의 한 어리석은 장수보다는 당장 옆 반 반장의 궁지가 더 즐거웠다. 불길한 낌새를 눈치 챈 선생이 웃음을 거두고 학생이 문 두드린 용건을 물었다.

　"수업을 끝내고 학생들을 귀가하시랍니다."

　"물론이지. 수업이 끝나면 학생들은 귀가하신다."

sang Province, Won Kyun, and his underhanded schemes and strategies had brought about the hero, Yi Sun-sin's ruin. *Ratatat. Ratatat. Ratatat.* The sound of the marbles didn't stop. There was nothing strange about it. No one in the classroom was playing with marbles.

There was a knock at the classroom door. Mr. Yi ignored the sound of marbles or the far-off thunder or whatever it was, and was getting ready to excite the students again about the 350-year-old story. He dropped his arms. He grinned, resigned, and went to open the door. It was the class monitor from next class.

"Are *you* Won Kyun?" Mr. Yi demanded, pointing an accusing finger at the puzzled boy's face. The class erupted with laughter. It was not clear if it had been the teacher's dramatic gesture or the boy's stunned reaction the class found funny. The teacher, assuming it was the former, beamed triumphantly, while the students laughed even harder because it had really been the latter. They delighted more in the distress of the class monitor from next door than in the demise of the foolish commander from 350 years ago. Sensing something important, the teacher stopped laughing and asked

학생들 사이에 또 웃음이 터졌다. 이번에는 선생의 재치 때문이었다. 그들은 수업 단축령이 떨어졌다는 것을 알았다. 그들이 알아차린 것을 선생이 모를 리 없었다. 그들은 선생이 그것을 안다는 것을 알았다. 그들도 선생과 마찬가지로 화가 났다. 그들은 하나도 즐겁지 않았다. 수업을 빼먹은 것이 안 즐거운 것이 아니었다. 그것은 많이 빼먹을수록 좋았다. 그들은 놀면 놀수록 더 놀고 싶었다. 놀 것은 얼마든지 있었다. 안 좋은 것은 수업 대신에 그들에게 떨어지는 것이 수업보다 더 나쁜 것이라는 점이었다. 깍쟁이 같은 어른들이 그들을 공부할 시간에 거저 놀려줄 리가 없었다. 공부시간은커녕 노는 시간에도 안 놀려주었다. 그들에게는 노는 시간이 없었다. 나중 그들이 어른이 되면, 그들은 우선 그들부터 실컷 놀고, 어린이들도 마음껏 뛰어놀게 해줄 참이었다. 놀면 밥은 누가 멕여 주나? 개미와 베짱이 이야기도 모르냐? 여름내 제금만 켜고 있으면, 겨울에 굶어 죽는다. 학생들이 수업 대신에 하는 일은 밥벌이나 겨우살이 준비가 아니었다. 그들은 서울서 높은 사람이 온다고 머나먼 기차역에 나가서 줄을 짓고 한없이 기다렸다. 그 높은 사람은 그들을 보러 오는 것이 아니었고, 그

the boy what he needed.

"I was told to let you know that the students should be dismissed after this class."

"Of course the students will be dismissed after class!"

The students burst into laughter again, this time at the teacher's wit. The students knew that the class monitor meant today would be a half day, and the teacher hadn't missed what the students noticed. The students also knew that the teacher knew. They were as frustrated by this as the teacher. They were not happy. The half day was not the problem. They liked to play, and the more they played, the more they wanted to go on playing. There were so many games to play. The students were unhappy because they knew that something worse than class was about to happen to them. The selfish adults would never cancel class to let the children play. The adults never let them play during playtime. The students had no time to play. The students planned to play when they became adults and then when they had children of their own, planned to let their children play to their hearts' content as well. If you play, who's going to put food on the table? Don't you know the story of

들이 알아듣는 말을 하는 사람도 아니었다. 그들은 가장 재미없는 수업보다 더 지루한 그의 긴 연설을 견디며 몸을 비비 꼬다가 해어진 운동화 끝으로 땅바닥에 금을 긋고 옆엣동무 옆구리를 찌르며 킬킬거리다 들켜서 무자비한 짝눈한테 솥뚜껑 같은 손바닥으로 뒷덜미를 철썩 소리가 나게 얻어맞았다. 등짝이 얼얼하게 아프기도 하려니와, 동네방네 소문나고 웃음거리 놀림감에, 별명 빌미 될까보아 창피하고 분한 맘에, 닭똥 같은 물방울이 두 눈에서 떨어졌다. 그것은 분명 밥벌이가 아니었다. 적어도 어린 그들의 밥벌이는 아니었다. 장광설이나 폭력은 어른들의 벌이고 놀이였다.

벌이가 안 되는 것은 그 밖에도 많았다. 줄 서서 기다리기 못지않게 열 지어 걸어가기도 그들이 원하는 바가 아니었다. 그것은 벌이도 놀이도 아니었다. 그들은 노래를 부르며 구호를 외치며 거리를 누볐다. 그것은 어른들의 밥벌이였고 놀이였다. 차라리 풀 뽑기, 땅 파기, 흙 나르기가 벌이에 더 가까웠다. 영화를 보는 것도 수업보다 별로 더 재미있지 않았다. 그것은 밤에 몰래 보는 것과 그렇게도 달랐다. 밤에 영화관에 가다가 들키면 정학이었다. 재미없고 사람을 시퍼보는 낮 영화는

14

the ant and the grasshopper? If you sing all summer, you'll starve in the winter. But the students weren't being pulled out of class to earn a living or to stock up for the winter. They were being herded out to the train station miles away to wait endlessly in rows for some important person from Seoul to arrive. The important people were never there to see the children, and never said anything the children could understand. The children endured the long speeches that were more tiresome than their most boring classes. They wriggled and squirmed, drew lines in the ground with the toes of their worn-out sneakers, poked their friends, giggled, got caught by the merciless cross-eyed teacher, and got slapped on the back with hands the size of pot lids. Their backs throbbing with pain, embarrassed and angry that everyone in the village would find out and make fun of them, the boys would cry, big wet drops. Tirades and violence were the occupation and source of entertainment for adults.

There were many other things that would not help them earn a living. They hated marching in rows just as much as they hated waiting in rows. It was neither work nor play. They sang songs and

어른들의 벌이였다. "오월이 푸르다. 들판에서 놀아라", "하늘이 높다. 산에 가서 놀아라", 또는 단순히 "날씨가 좋다. 나가 놀아라"고 하면 어른들의 벌이가 안 되었다.

그들한테서 웃음이 터진 것은 역사 선생이 뻔히 알면서 시치미를 뗀 것이 그들의 기분에 맞았기 때문이었다. 그것은 수업 단축에 대한 강한 불만의 표시였다. 심부름 온 학생에게 그 이상 화풀이를 할 수는 없었다. 옆반 반장을 보낸 선생은 교단으로 돌아와서, "자, 여러분. 수군대첩은 다음 시간에 또 듣자. 오늘은 이만하고, 지금 당장 책보를 싸가지고 집으로들 간다. 청소도 하지 마라. 무슨 일인지는 나도 모르겠다"고 말했다. 그 소리가 조금 비장했다.

"안 됩니다. 담임한테 혼납니다. 뚜드러 맞습니다."

"괜찮다. 느그 담임 부탁이다."

그들은 아침나절 공부도 다 못 하고 학교를 파했다. 구슬 굴리는 소리로 들렸던 것은 멀리 기차역 쪽에서 났다. 그것은 먼 천둥소리도 아니었다. 가을하늘이 너무 맑았다. 그 소리는 점점 시내 쪽으로 다가왔다. 가까워질수록 낮고 둔한 울림이 없어지고, 딱딱하고 날카로운 찢어지는 소리가 났다. 그것은 그의 집을 지나, 해가 설핏

marched through the streets chanting slogans. But these were the adults' ideas of work and play. Weeding, digging ditches, and transporting dirt would have felt more like work.

Watching movies was no better than being in class. It was so different from sneaking into the theatre at night to watch movies. You could get suspended from school for getting caught at a movie theatre at night.

The daytime features, boring and patronizing, were also adults' work. Adults could not earn a living telling children, "In the merry month of May, go out to the fields and play," or "The sky is high. Over the green meadows, fly." Or even "It's nice out. Go out and play."

The students laughed because the teacher's feigned ignorance of the class monitor's message suited the students' frustration regarding the whole affair. By playing dumb, he was protesting the half day. But he could not take it out on the student messenger any more than he already had. The teacher sent the student back to his class, returned to his podium, and said, "Children, we'll learn more about the Battle of Hansan Island next class. We'll stop here today. Pack your bags immediately and

할 무렵에 시내 경찰서 쪽에서 콩 볶는 시늉을 했다.

"감 따먹자."

"죽고 싶냐?"

"엎드려서 기어가지."

"나무 위에 올라가면 엎드려도 소양없다."

"장끄방에 찰싹 붙어 간짓대로 따면 되지."

"그것 하로 안 먹으면 몸이 어디 어긋나냐? 감이라고 허는 것은 안 먹어도 안 죽는다. 당장 병원 가야 허는 죽어가는 중환자도, 집중사격 한복판을 어디라고 꼼짝 허냐?"

"성도 감은 먹고 싶지?"

"십자포화 생각하면 먹은 감도 넘어온다. 군것질도 체면 있지, 배고프면 밥 먹어라."

"아무 때나 밥을 묵어? 밥 배 따로 감 배 따로."

"급헐 때는 급헌 대로 참을 것은 참고 살아."

"총소리만 안 난다면 급헐 것이 하나 없다."

"말이라고."

"소리가 무섭냐?"

"그것이 그냥 나냐?"

"소리 안 나는 총이 있으면 좋겠다."

go home. Don't clean the classroom. I don't know what's going on either." He put up a brave front.

"No, sir. We have to clean. We'll get a sound beating from our homeroom teacher."

"It's okay. This came straight from your teacher."

They were dismissed before the morning classes were through. The marble sounds were coming from far away, from the direction of the train station. But it wasn't thunder. The autumn sky was too clear for thunder. The sound moved downtown. The closer it came, the harder and sharper it grew as the low, muffled rings echoed througout the village and dissipated. The sound moved past the boy's house and by dusk sounded like beans roasting near the downtown police station.

"Let's pick some persimmons."

"Do you want to die?"

"We'll crawl there."

"It's no use when you're in the trees."

"We'll stay close to the crocks and get 'em with poles."

"It won't kill you if you don't eat persimmons for one day. Even if you're a dying patient and you need to get to the hospital right away, you can't run through a converging fire."

"뭘 하게?"

"죽을 때 죽더라도 죽을 때까지는 죽는 줄 모르게."

"소문 없이 죽는 것이 뭣이 좋냐? 급살 맞으면 짹 소리도 못 하고 죽는다."

"구신한테 홀렸냐?"

"귀신이 물어가고 도깨비가 업어갔으면 덜 억울하다. 자객은 소리 없이 찌르고, 암살자는 총을 쏴도 소음기를 쓴다."

"소음기가 뭣이냐? 시끄럽게 하는 기계냐?"

"멍청이. 시끄러우면 어찌 쥐도 새도 모르게 죽이냐? 소리를 죽이는 장치다."

"비겁하다. 사람을 몰래 죽일라고 소리부터 먼저 죽이냐?"

"그래. 그것이 소리 없는 총이다."

"그런 것 말고. 앞에서 알게 쏘는 소리 없는 총."

"미운 놈 뒤꼭지 쏠라면 소리가 안 나야 안 들켜, 바보야. 앞에서 쏠라면 소리가 나거나말거나."

"소리가 나면 시끄러워서 정신이 없어. 마지막 가는 길 정중히 보내면 안 되냐? 쏘는 사람한테 밉다고 다 밉냐, 쏘는 놈 맘대로?"

"But you do want persimmons, don't you?"

"When I think of crossfires, I can feel every persimmon I've eaten in my life come right back up. There's a time and place for snacking. If you're hungry, have some rice."

"It's not dinner time yet. Besides, I have a separate stomach for persimmons."

"When things are rough, you gotta give up a few things."

"Things wouldn't be rough if I didn't have to hear the guns all the time."

"Right."

"Are you afraid of the sound?"

"It's not the sound I'm afraid of. It's what comes with it."

"I wish they had guns that didn't make sounds."

"For what?"

"So when you die, you won't know that you are about to die."

"What's so great about dying without warning? If they get you in a vital point, drop dead without so much as a peep."

"You're talking about this like you just saw a ghost."

"I'd prefer a ghost or the devil any day. Assassins

"쏠 때는 쏘는 놈 맘이지 맞는 놈 맘이냐, 바보야?"

"참, 성도. 죽는 것은 쏘는 놈이 아니라 맞는 놈인디."

"너하고 말하면 배고파."

"감 묵자."

"죽을 놈보고 죽을라냐고 물으면 죽겠다고 헐 놈이 어디 있냐?"

"그렇다고 쏠 놈 맘대로 쏘나? 죽을 놈이 죽을죄를 지었다고 고백해도 함부로 못 쏠 텐디."

"총소리가 좀 뜸해졌냐?"

"군인하고 순경하고 싸우면 누가 이기냐?"

"군대하고 경찰하고 싸우면 군대가 이긴다. 수가 많거든."

"같은 수면?"

"그래도 군인이 이긴다. 장닭은 한 본 이기면 항상 이긴다."

"우리들하고 같냐? 우리도 한 본 지면 항상 진다."

"다 싸워봤냐, 육십 명하고?"

"아니."

"어떻게 아냐? 다 아냐?"

"그래도 알어. 다 알어. 분명하지 않을 때만 싸워."

slit your throat without making a sound and they use silencers on their guns."

"What's a silencer? Does it silence people?"

"Why would you want to silence *people*? It silences the *gun*."

"That's cowardly, to first kill the sound to kill a person."

"That's what the silencer is for."

"I don't want something like that. I want a silent gun you shoot from the front."

"If you're going to shoot a villain from behind, you need a silent gun so you don't get caught. If you're going to shoot from the front, who cares if you make a sound or not?"

"The sound distracts you. You should be respectful of the person who's about to die. Not everyone's a villain who's been bad to the shooter. Shooting shouldn't be about the shooter."

"When someone's shooting, the shooter is in control, idiot. Not the one who's getting shot."

"Well, it's the one who's being shot that's going to die. Not the shooter."

"Talking to you makes me hungry."

"Let's have persimmons."

"No one says yes when you ask them if they want

"처음에는?"

"처음부터 분명해. 분명치 않을 때가 드물어. 일주일에 한 번. 한 달에 두어 번."

"맨 처음. 처음 만났을 때. 한 본도 안 싸웠을 때. 학기 초. 안 싸우고 아냐?"

"알어. 조금씩 분명해져서 나중에는 다 분명해. 학기 도중에 전학 온 아도 육십 명하고 한 본씩 육십 번 싸울 필요 없어. 한두 번 토닥거려보면 자리 매김 끝나."

"그 아야 순번이 정해진 다음에 끼여들어서 자리 찾기가 쉬웠지. 순서가 아예 없는 처음. 반 편성이 막 끝났을 때."

"일학년 때까지 거슬러 올라가냐? 소문이 나고 조금씩 싸우고 싸운 것이 또 소문나고, 그러면 어느새 순번이 매겨져, 정확하게. 병아리 새끼들이 털도 덜 난 날개로 땅을 짚고 두 발로 형제들의 앞가슴을 모주리 차례로 차고 튀어오르지. 우리들은 삐갱이 새끼들보다는 낫다."

"뭐가 낫냐? 조금씩 싸우는 것이 낫냐? 그것도 싸우는 것은 싸우는 것이지. 살살 때리냐?"

"그래. 살살 때려. 안 때리고 말만 하기도 하고. 말도 안 하고 쳐다보기만 하기도 하고. 그 지식이 쌓여. 우리

to die."

"That doesn't give you the right to shoot them. Even if the one who's about to be shot confesses that he deserves to be shot."

"I don't hear as much shooting anymore."

"If a soldier fights a cop, who wins?"

"If an army fights the police, the army wins. There are more of them."

"What if there's the same number on each side?"

"Still, the soldiers win. Once the strongest kid at our school wins, he keeps winning."

"They're not the same as us. When one of us loses, we keep losing."

"Have you fought with everyone? All sixty kids in your class?"

"No."

"So how do you know? You don't know everything."

"I do too. I know. They only fight when they're not sure."

"What about in the beginning?"

"At first, it's a sure thing. You're only occasionally not sure. Once a week. Maybe once or twice a month."

"What about way in the beginning? When you

들의 머리통이 병아리들의 것보다는 크다."

"병아리 대가리가 얼마나 큰디? 엄지발가락만한 것보다 더 큰 것도 자랑이냐? 비슷한 것하고 비교해라."

"무엇하고 비슷하냐?"

"무엇이? 두 개가 있어야 비슷하지."

"어른하고 어린이하고 같냐?"

"다르다."

"얼마나 다르냐? 병아리보다 더 다르냐?"

"사람하고 짐승하고 같냐?"

"헤집기 잘하는 새만 짐생이고, 머리 검은 짐생은 짐생 아니냐? 사람이면 다 같냐? 왜 금방 다르다고 했냐?"

"지금도 달라. 닭의 새끼보다는 같다만."

"닭의 새끼는 다르고 사람의 새끼는 같냐?"

"아니. 닭의 새끼들도 즈그들끼리는 같고, 사람의 새끼들도 딴 짐생의 새끼들허고는 다르다."

"사람도 즈그들끼리는 같냐? 어른하고 어린이는 같냐?"

"그래."

"내나 다르다고 해놓고."

"다를 때도 있고 같을 때도 있다. 다르다고 항상 다르

met for the first time. When you haven't fought at all. In the beginning of the semester. How do you know without fighting them if you're going to win?"

"I know. It becomes clear little by little and then later it's all clear. Someone who transfers in the middle of semester doesn't have to fight all sixty kids one by one. He just has to fight a few and then he knows where he ranks."

"That's *after* the order has been established. It's easy to find your place once the order is set, but what about in the very beginning when there is no order? Right after you're assigned to your new class."

"At this rate, you're going to ask me, 'What about in the first grade?' You find out through rumors about fights, and before you know it, we have an order. A precise order. Even a chick without all its feathers in knows to get up higher by jump on its brothers' backs. At least we're better than chicks."

"How are we better than chicks? Is it better if you don't fight so much? It's still fighting. It doesn't hurt any less."

"It does hurt less. Sometimes, we don't hit each other at all. We use words. Sometimes, we don't even use words. We stare at each other. That's how

고, 같다고 항상 같냐? 푼수."

"다른 것하고 같은 것하고 뜻이 같은갑다. 다른 것이 같고, 같은 것이 다른갑다."

"그래. 다른 것에 비하면 같고, 같은 것에 비하면 달라. 어린이와 병아리가 같을 때도 있고, 어린이와 어른이 같을 때도 있어. 다를 때도 있고."

"어른하고 병아리도 같냐?

"그래. 같어."

"아니, 아니. 다르냐?"

"그래. 달러."

"미련하고 잘 싸우는 것은 같다, 셋 다."

"그래."

"셋 중에서 누가 가장 멍청헌 싸납쟁이냐? 삥아리냐?"

"아니."

"사람이냐? 사람 중에서도 어른이냐?"

"그래. 어른이 제일 싸나운 멍청이. 어른하고 어린이는 병아리하고 같으면 바보, 어른은 어린이하고 같으면 바보."

"그것이 다른갑다. 병아리는 사람하고 같으면 영리하냐? 어린이는 어른하고 같으면 똑똑하냐?"

28

you build reputations. Our heads are bigger compared to chicks."

"Chicks' heads aren't so big. Having a head larger than your big toe is nothing to be proud of. Pick something your own size."

"What's close?"

"What's *closer*? You need two things to compare."

"How about kids and adults? Are they similar?"

"No."

"How different? More different than kids and chicks?"

"How can animals and people be more similar?"

"Birds who peck are animals, but animals with black hair aren't animals? Not all people are the same. Didn't you just say people are different?"

"It's still different. Less different than people and baby chickens, though."

"Baby chickens are different but baby people are the same?"

"No, baby chickens are similar to adult chickens, but baby people are different from other baby animals."

"Are people similar? Adults and kids?"

"Yes."

"You said they were different."

"그래. 그 말이 그 말이여."

"어째서 그 말이 그 말이냐? 어째서 가장 멍청한 것하고 같으면 영리허냐?"

"같고 다르고 둘 다 한꺼번에 헐라면 그럴 수밖에 더 있냐? 사람새끼는 아무리 현명해도 멍청하고, 닭의 새끼는 아무리 멍청해도 현명하다."

"현명한 사람이 멍청한 닭만 못허냐?"

"왜 사람이 미물만 못하냐?"

"병아리는 왜 싸우고, 사람은 왜 싸우냐? 다르냐?"

"같어. 싸납쟁이니까 싸워."

"왜 싸납쟁이냐?"

"싸우니까 싸납쟁이야."

"바보. 바보니까 싸우지."

"그래. 싸우니까 바보고."

"부리허고 발톱으로 할쿠는 것하고, 주먹허고 발로 치고 박는 것허고, 총허고 칼로 지지고 찌르는 것허고, 다 같냐?"

"다 같어. 다 싸움인디."

"엉덩방아 찧는 것허고, 눈텡이에 퍼렁멍 드는 것허고, 피범벅이 되어 땅바닥을 뽁뽁 기는 것허고, 다 같냐?"

"Sometimes they're similar and sometimes they're not. Things can't be different all the time, and things can't be the same all the time, either. Idiot."

"I guess 'different' and 'same' mean the same thing. Different things are the same, and the same things are different."

"Yes, they're the same compared to different ones, and different compared to the same ones. Sometimes, children and chicks are the same, and sometimes kids and adults are the same—or different."

"Are adults and chicks the same?"

"Yes, they are."

"No, I mean... are they different?"

"They're different."

"They're all the same because they're all fools and like to fight."

"Yes."

"Which one is the stupidest and most violent? The chicks?"

"No."

"People? Adults?"

"Yes. Adults are the biggest violent idiots. Adults and kids are stupid if they act like chicks, and adults are stupid if they act like kids."

"같어. 죽기 아니면 살기지."

"죽고 사는 것이 같냐?"

"그것들만 빼고 같어."

"싸움에서 죽고 사는 것 빼고 나면 뭣이 남냐?"

"싸움이 남지. 죽을 데까지 가는 것은 죽지만 않았을 뿐이지, 죽은 것과 무엇이 다르냐?"

"아무리 그래도 죽는 것하고 사는 것하고 같냐?"

"죽는 것만 못한 사는 것이 있고, 사는 것보다 더한 죽는 것도 있어. 같은 것은 아무것도 아니여."

"같다면 더하고 못할 것이 뭣이냐?"

"그것들 안 빼고도 같어. 뒤로 자빠져도 죽을라면 죽고, 땅바닥을 기어도 살라면 살어. 싸움은 삥아리 삐약삐약 싸움이건, 어린이들 티각태각 싸움이건, 어른들 쿵쾅쿵쾅 싸움이건, 다 같어. 모든 싸움은 다 같어, 죽든 살든."

"죽든 살든 같으면, 안 죽으면 더 같냐? 옛날이건 요새건, 먼 데건 가까운 데건, 크건 작건, 쳐들어가건 막건, 이기건 지건, 얻건 잃건, 다 같냐? 같은 것이 다르고 다른 것이 같다면 같아봤자냐?"

"제갈량 싸움이 양산박 싸움허고 같고, 그것들이 살수

"I guess that's what's different. If chicks act like people, aren't they smart? But are kids who act like adults smart?"

"Yes, that's the same thing."

"How is that the same thing? How come if you're the same as the stupidest animal, you're smart?"

"You can't help it if you're the same and different at the same time. Baby people are stupid no matter how smart they get, and baby chicken are smart no matter how stupid they get."

"Why is a smart man no better than a dumb chicken?"

"Why are people no better than animals?"

"Why do chicks fight, and why do humans? Are the reasons different?"

"The reasons are the same. They fight because they're violent."

"Why are they violent?"

"Because they fight."

"Idiot. They fight because they're idiots."

"Yes, and they're idiots because they fight."

"Is fighting with your claws and beaks the same as using your fists and feet? The same as using guns and swords? Are they all the same?"

"They're all the same. They're all fights."

대첩이나 임진왜란, 병자호란허고 같다. 또 그것들이
다 일본군 만주싸움이나 중국싸움이나 진주만싸움허
고 같다."

"요는 중국 사람들이나 조선 사람들이나 일본 사람들
이나 다 같다는 말이냐? 병아리들허고 어린이들은 어
찌고? 암탉들을 놓고 장닭들이 싸우는 것이 적벽대전
허고 같냐?"

"닭의 새끼들이 왜 싸우냐? 거름자리에서 땅 차지할
라고 싸운다. 조조허고 손권이 양자강에서 왜 싸웠냐?
유비허고 셋이서 천하를 삼분 헐라고 싸웠다."

"땅싸움이냐? 허기는 조국도 땅인갑다. 나라를 위하
여도 땅을 위하연갑다. 임진란 올돌목 수군대첩도 결국
땅싸움이냐?"

"그래. 비행기가 공중에서 싸우는 것도 땅싸움이여. 그
렇지만 두엄더미허고 천하대륙은 너무 차이난다, 그지?"

"그것은 걱정할 것 없어. 삥아리허고 어른허고 얼마나
차이 나냐?"

"그래? 괜찮냐? 그래도 광대한 중국 대륙이 너무 크다?"

"괜찮어. 안 커. 하느님이 높은 데서 내려다보면 중국
천하도 손바닥만할 거야. 공자가 태산만 올라도, 천하

"How about falling on your butt, getting a black eye, and getting all covered in blood and crawling on the ground? Are *those* all the same?"

"They're all the same. They're all either living or dead."

"Life and death are the same?"

"They're all the same except for that."

"If you take life and death out of fights, what's left?"

"The fight. Getting close to death is not different from dying, except that you're not actually dead."

"Still, how are dying and living the same?"

"There's life worse than death, and there's also death better than life. Life and death being the same is nothing compared to this."

"If they're the same, what's the use in comparing which one is better?"

"Even if you don't take life and death out of fights, fights are still all the same. Even if you fall on your butt, if you were meant to die, you'll die. Even if you're crawling on the ground, you'll live if you were meant to live. Fights are all the same, whether it's chicks going peep peep or kids going whim wham or adults going bang bang. All fights are the same, whether you live or die."

가 좁았다."

"그래. 사람이 병아리 시퍼보면 하느님이 사람을 얼마
나 우습게 보겠냐?"

"사람이 닭의 새끼를 무시하면 닭의 새끼는 지렁이새
끼, 풍뎅이새끼, 거미새끼, 파리새끼를 얼마나 같잖게
여기냐? 발로 밟아버리고 주둥이로 쪼아버린다."

"개미는 닭이 다가오면 산이 움직인다고 허겄다."

"유식헌 개미나 그러지, 보통 일개미는 무엇이 오는지
나 알어?"

"박식한 개미들도 의견이 분분허겄다. 두 번째 개미는
하늘이 무너진다고 허고, 세 번째 개미는 땅이 꺼진다
고 허고, 닭의 새끼 한 마리가 오는디. 히, 히."

"웃지 마. 땅이 꺼지고 하늘이 무너지고는 사람들 문
자여. 개미들헌테 물어보도 않고."

"누가 개미들 때문에 웃냐? 없는 디서 좀 웃으면 안
되냐? 그럴 때 개미들이 웃는지 우는지 어떻게 아냐?
개미들도 웃을 줄 아냐?"

"그럼 무엇 때문에 웃었냐?"

"사람들 때문에 웃었다. 곰은 미련하고 여우는 간사하
냐? 북극 얼음바다에서 얼어 죽지 않고 겨울을 나는 곰

"If they're the same if you live or die, is it more same if you don't die? If it was in the past or now, close or faraway, big or small, whether you attack or are attacked, win or lose, gain or lose—are they all the same? If same is different and different is the same, what does it matter if it's the same or not?"

"Zhuge Liang's war is the same as the war in Liangshan Marsh, and they're the same as the Battle of Salsu, the Imjin War, and the Manchu Invasion. And they're all the same as wars in Japan, Manchu, China, and Pearl Harbor."[1]

"In other words, are you saying that the Chinese, Japanese, and Koreans are all the same? What about chicks and kids? How are roosters fighting over hens the same thing as the Battle of Red Cliffs?"[2]

"Why do baby chickens fight? They fight to have more space in the coop. Why did Cao Cao and Sun Quan fight at the Yangtze? They fought to divide up the world into three with Liu Bei."

"So it was a fight over land? I guess this land is land, too. Fighting for the country is fighting for land. So the war at sea during the Imjin War was also a fight over land?"

"Yes, airplanes fighting in the sky also fight over

이 왜 미련허냐? 여우가 사냥꾼의 냄새 잘 맡는 사냥개의 송곳니한테 목덜미를 내놓지 않아서 간사하냐? 그것 다 사람들 이야기여. 야, 개미헌테 닭이 사람헌테 없겠냐?"

"사람들도 개미들겉이 속도 모르고 물색없이 뚱딴지겉은 소리 허냐?"

"그래. 개미들 하나 안 우스워. 사람들 때문에 우스워. 사실, 개미는 사람들겉이 그렇게 미련하지 않는 모양이더라. 적어도 사람들이 생각하는 것만큼 미련하지는 않는 모양이더라. 개미는 장마가 들고, 홍수가 나고, 큰물이 질 것을 미리 안다더라."

"개미들이? 그 고자 수염 겉은 더듬이로?"

"사람들이 태양계, 은하계 가지고 노는 것에 대면 아무것도 아니지."

"아무것이지. 알도 못허는 은하계가 무슨 소용이냐, 내일 비가 올지 맑을지도 모름서? 개미들은 알 것은 안다. 큰비 올 것을 알다니, 내, 참, 그 쪼깐헌 것들이 웃긴다. 작은비는 집이 튼튼해서 몰라도 문제없단 말이지? 아, 큰비 오면 사람 집도 떠내려가는디, 개미굴 성허냐? 사람들은 제 집 떠내려갈 큰비는커녕, 원족 망칠 작은

land. But the coop and the world are too different, aren't they?"

"Don't worry about that. Chicks and adults aren't that different."

"Really? It's okay? But China's so big."

"It's not that big. If God looked down on earth, China would be the size of his palm. Confucius only had to climb a hill to see how small the world was."

"True. Just as people think chicks are insignificant, God probably also thinks people are nothing."

"If people think chicks are worthless, guess how chicks think about baby worms, baby beetles, baby spiders, and baby flies. They stomp on them and peck at them with their beaks."

"When an ant sees a chicken coming toward it, it probably thinks a mountain is moving."

"Smart ants would think that. Average worker ants wouldn't even notice."

"The smart ants will get into a big debate about it. One ant will say the sky is falling, and another will say the earth is giving out beneath. And all the while it's only a baby chicken. Hehe."

"Don't laugh. Only people think that the sky is falling or the earth is opening up. You don't know

비도 몰라."

"군인들이 왜 순사들헌테 총질 허냐?"

"진짜 쏘았냐?"

"그래. 봤어. 논두럭길로 오는디 어디서, 학생, 비껴,
하는 소리가 나서 깜짝 놀라 멈췄더니, 나락 사이로 내
민 총구가, 타당 타다당, 하고 불을 뿜었다. 군인이 철모
밑으로 얼굴을 내밀고 총을 쏘고도 시침을 뚝 떼고 엎
드려 있더라. 우리들은 교복 웃웃을 벗어 들고 왔다. 경
찰들하고 혼동허지 말라고."

"총구에서 연기가 나더냐?"

"그래. 불이 뻔쩍 했다."

"대낮인디 불빛이 보이냐? 한 본만 뻔쩍 했냐, 소리는
여러 본 나고?"

"뻔쩍뻔쩍 했다. 소리가 여러 본인디 불이 한 본이겄
냐?"

"경찰도 웃웃을 벗으면 되겄다."

"바보야, 우리는 선생님들이 군인들하고 협상을 맺었
다. 깜정 옷 입었다고 다 경찰이 아니다. 학생들도 교복
이 검정이다. 상의를 벗어 들고 귀가하게 해라."

"군대가 학교에 들어왔냐? 선생들하고는 안 싸웠냐? 경

anything about what ants think."

"I'm not laughing because of the ants. What does it matter if I laugh behind their backs anyway? How do *you* know if ants cry or laugh over these things? Can ants laugh?"

"So then what did you laugh for?"

"I laughed because people are funny. Are bears foolish and foxes wily? Could bears survive the icy winter at the North Pole if they were foolish? Are foxes wily because they're clever enough to escape the fangs of the hunting dogs? These are all things people made up. Ants talk about chickens the way people talk about animals."

"So people just say things without knowing what the truth is? Like ants?"

"Yes. I wasn't laughing at the ants. I was laughing at people. Actually, ants aren't as foolish as people think. I hear ants can predict monsoons, floods, and tides."

"They can? With their tiny little antennas?"

"It's nothing compared to people who explore the solar system and galaxy."

"It *is* something. What's the use of knowing about galaxies if you can't predict whether or not it's going to rain tomorrow? Ants know what's important.

찰들도 웃옷을 벗으면 학생들은 바지까지 벗어야겠다?"

"그 비밀이 샜을 때쯤이면, 전쟁이 끝났거나 학생들이 다 집에 도착했다."

"전쟁이 그렇게 빨리 끝나냐? 벌써 끝났는갑다, 총소리가 안 나는 것을 보니."

"감 따올래?"

그들은 밖으로 나갔다. 그의 머릿속에는 그의 형이 본 불을 뿜는 숨겨진 총부리가 깊은 인상을 남겼다. 그는 감이 먹고 싶은 그 자신을 이해할 수 없었다. 감? 감이라니? 감이 어디서 감히. 부모의 금족령을 어기고 몰래 고샅을 빠져나가 총알이 날아다니는 격전지를 정찰해도 부족할 때에 한가로이 과실이나 따먹고 앉았다니. 그는 그 무렵 팔일삼의 비밀을 읽고 있었다. 팔일삼을 합하면 열둘이 되고, 열두 시에 사건이 터진다는 탐정소설이었다. 연애소설들도 비슷한 수준들이었다. 여학생의 정조, 검사와 여선생. 어른들은 딴 일들에 바빠서 아이들의 읽을거리에 신경을 쓸 틈이 없었다. 아이들은 어른들 책들을 읽었다. 그것들은 그들이 보기에도 유치했다. 즉 그들에게 알맞았다. 그들은 그것들을 돌려가며 탐독했다. 어른들은 어른들 책들 돌볼 틈도 없었다.

Those little fellas are amazing, knowing when a big rain is coming. I guess little showers are okay because it won't wash their houses away. Big rains wash peoples' houses away, so the ants' houses won't be safe. People can't predict big rains that'll wash their houses away, let alone little ones that spoil picnics."

"Why are the soldiers shooting at the policemen?"

"Did they really shoot?"

"Yes, I saw it. I was coming home along the paddy when I heard, 'Kid, get out of the way!' I froze right there, and a muzzle appeared out of the wheat and spat fire. Ping! Ping! The soldier lay still under his helmet and pretended nothing happened. We took off our shirts so they wouldn't mistake us for policemen."

"Did you see smoke coming from the muzzle?"

"Yes. There were sparks."

"You saw sparks during the day? Did the gun flash? Did you hear a couple gunshots?"

"It went flash flash. How can there be one flash when there's more than one gunshots?"

"I guess the police could try taking their shirts off, too."

"Idiot. The teachers made an agreement with the

그들은 정치하랴, 장사하랴, 정신들이 없었다. 그들의 마음은 늦되어 어린이들의 마음과 같았고, 어린이들은 올되어 어른과 같았다. 어른들은 어린이들처럼 덜되었고, 어린이들은 어른들처럼 겉늙었다. 둘 다 불행이었다. 어른들이 어른 노릇과 어린이 노릇을 하고, 어린이들이 어린이 노릇과 어른 노릇을 하는 것은 둘 중 누구도 두 노릇들 중 어느 하나 제대로 못하는 것이었다. 어린이 세계에 머물러 있는 어른도 볼품없지만, 어른 세계에 뛰어든 어린이도 볼썽사나웠다. 있어야 할 곳에 있지 않는 잘못은 반드시 있지 않아야 할 곳에 있는 잘못과 맞물려 두 가지 죄를 저질렀다. 어린이들이 없고 어른들이 없었다. 어린이들은 어른 행세를 해서 어린이를 없앴고, 어른들은 어린이 짓을 해서 어른을 없앴다. 진짜는 사라지고 가짜가 생겼다. 어린이 아닌 어린이는 어린이가 아니었고, 어른 아닌 어른은 어른이 아니었다. 어른과 어린이로 된 세상에서 어른과 어린이가 없으면 무엇이 남는가? 짐승. 살아남기 위해서 사는 짐승이 있었다. 어린이들은 등에 계란껍질 조각들을 짊어진 채 아직 덜 마른 털을 털며 비틀비틀 걷는 병아리들처럼, 처음으로 눈을 뜨자마자 벼랑으로 떨어지는 사자새

soldiers for us. 'Not everyone in black shirts are policemen. Students wear black shirts, too. Then tell them to take off their shirts on their way home.'"

"Did the soldiers come into the school? They didn't fight with the teachers? If the policemen start taking off their shirts, too, I guess students will have to take off their pants."

"By the time that secret gets out, the war'll be over, or the students will have all gone back home."

"Wars don't end that quickly! Do you think it's over now just because we don't hear any gunshots right now?"

"Do you want to go get persimmons?"

They went. The fire-spitting muzzle that his older brother saw had left a deep impression on him. He did not understand his own desire to eat persimmons. Persimmons? Persimmons! Impermissible! He should have been out disobeying his parents' orders not to leave the house, sneaking out the alley, and doing recon of the battlefield where the bullets were flying. But despite the grave circumstances, he was picking and eating fruit without a care in the world.

끼들처럼, 걸음마를 다 배우기도 전에 먹이사냥에 나서거나 굶거나 했고, 어른들은 아량, 양보, 염치, 이상 같은 것들을 생전 보도 듣도 못해서 굶주리고 병든 들짐 승들처럼 제 새끼도 못 알아보았다. 달라야 보였다. 그들은 그들의 모습을 몰랐다. 비춰볼 거울이 없었다. 그들은 서로에게서 그들의 모습을 보았다, 어른들은 아이들에게서, 아이들은 어른들에게서. 신문은 아마 있었다. 두 쪽들이나 네 쪽들이었을 것이다. 방송도 있었지만, 그것을 들을 수 있는 기구는 운이 좋아야 동네에 하나 정도였다. 그의 집에는 없었다. 그의 집에 축음기는 있었다. 개가 확성기 앞에 앉아 있는 상표였다. 문제는 판이었다. 비 내리는 고모령인가 하고 "분단장 주름살에 눈물이 어려 아들 짜 떼버리면 세상도 없"손가 하는 것하고, 그 비슷한 노래들뿐이었다. 요즘 유행하는 가요 가장 좋은 것 열 개가 모두 남녀 간의 상열지사인 것처럼, 그때는 어머니와 자식 사이의 정, 그것도 유복하고 정상적인 것보다는 끊어지고 불쌍한 정을 노래하는 것들이었다. 그것은 사람의 느낌들 중에서 가장 먼저고 가장 깊은 것이어서 거의 짐승 같았다. 특히 불행한 것이 그랬다. 그것은 문화라든가 인공이라든가 전통이라

He had been reading about the secret of 813. He had learned that if you added eight, one, and three, you got twelve, and that meant a crime would take place at twelve. He'd read it in a detective novel. Romance novels weren't any better. The chaste schoolgirl. The inspector. The female teacher. Adults were too busy to care what children were reading. Children read books for adults. Even children found them childish. In other words, the books were perfect for the children. The books were passed around amongst the children. Adults were too busy to read adult books. They were busy with politics and business. Their minds were immature like children's, and children's minds were mature like adults.' The adults were immature like children, and the children were mature like adults. This was a tragedy for everyone. Adults acting like adults and children. Children acting like children and adults. This meant that neither could do a good job of being either. Adults being childish was unseemly, but children in the world of adults was ghastly. The crime of not being where one should be, mixed with the crime of being where one should not be. It was two crimes at once. There were no children, and there were no adults. Chil-

든가 관습이라든가 하는 것들에 길들여지지 않고, 자연, 숲, 원시, 벗음 같은 것들로 돌아갔다. 아, 그때 판소리 열두 마당, 아니, 다섯 마당이 있었더라면 얼마나 좋았을까! 육자배기가 한숨 반, 가락 반으로 근근히 부지깽이나 지게목발 장단에 맞춰 명맥을 이었다. 정월 보름 큰 명절에 온 동네를 돌아가며 집집마다 잡귀 잡고 악귀 쫓는 농악이나, 촌에 가면 동구마다 철 따라서 옷 바꾸고 신선처럼 장엄하게 동네 평안 지켜주는 당산나무, 당산굿은 무당굿에 장승이라, 미련한 민족의 미개한 미신이었다. 일찍 나라를 열고 서양을 받아들여 남먼저 개명한 섬사람들이 삼십여 년에 걸쳐 끈질기게 식민지를 가꾼 덕분에 옛것은 그런대로 분탕질이 되었고, 더러 모진 목숨이 질겨서 숨이 덜 끊어졌으면 천민층 속으로 자취를 감췄다. 상놈들은 그런대로 묵은 것 덜 버린 것으로 연명을 했다. 목숨을 부지했을 뿐만 아니라 위에서 밑으로 밑으로 잦아드는 바람에 저변이 확대되었다. 허공에 붕 뜬 것은 서둘러 헌것을 버린 양반들이었다. 난쟁이들의 치밀하고 집요한 노고에도 불구하고 야만의 땅에서 헌것 새것 물갈이는 마무리가 덜 되었다. 새것은 아직 하층까지 미치지 못했고, 상층에도

48

dren acted like adults, thereby eliminating children. Adults acted like children, thereby eliminating adults. The real disappeared and the fake emerged. Children who were not children were not children, and adults who were not adults were not adults. In a world made of adults and children, what remains when adults and children disappear? Animals. Animals living just to survive. Like baby chicks taking their first wobbly steps, eggshells still clinging to their backs, and like lion cubs tumbling down hills the second they open their eyes for the first time, children were going out hunting or starving before they were learning to walk. Like starved, diseased wild beasts who had not yet learned compassion, generosity, or how to listen to the voices of their conscience, the adults did not recognize their young. They had to be different to recognize each other. They did not even know what they themselves looked like. There were no mirrors. They saw themselves in each other, adults in children, children in adults.

I suppose there were newspapers. Two-page or four-page papers. There were radio announcements, too, but a village was lucky if they had one radio to share amongst all of them. There was no

뿌리를 내리지 못했다. 문화적 공백이었다. 영화나 자동차는 그렇다 치고 연극 무용, 음악 미술, 민속 전설, 심지어 문학 역사에 이르기까지, 문화 전반에 걸쳐서 새살림을 장만하지도 않고 묵은 세간을 내다버렸다. 새것 장만이 묵은 것 버리기였다. 다만, 새것이라고 신주까지 불 쳐지르면서 헐레벌떡 끌어안은 것이 말짱 헛것이고 가짜였다. 빌려 입고, 얻어 입고, 주워 입은 옷을 제 옷보다 더 나은 제 옷이라고 착각하고, 앞을 다투어 갈아입은 것이 잘못이었다. 갈아입은 것이 잘못이 아니라, 갈아입을 수 있다고, 또는 갈아입고도 아무 탈이 없을 것이라고, 탈이 있기는커녕 더 뱃속이 편할 것이라고 믿은 것이 잘못이었다. 문화에서 파괴는 창조에 의해서만 가능했다. 남의 옷 아무것이나 함부로 걸칠 수도 없거니와, 제 옷이라고 마음대로 벗어 던질 수도 없었다. 아무리 누더기라도 갈아입을 옷 없이 벗어 던지는 것은, 그럴 수 있다 하더라도, 미친 짓이었고, 그보다 더 미친 것은 누더기를 걸치고 있으면서 단지 그것을 싫어한다는 이유만으로 그것을 벗고 새옷을 입었다고 믿는 것이었다. 입고 있는 옷이 걸레라도 그랬다. 그것은 걸레가 아니었다. 오래 되었으니 걸레냐? 살가죽도

radio at his house. There was a gramophone in-stead. It bore a logo of a dog sitting in front of a gramophone. The problem was the records. All they had was "Rainy Komoryeong" and another song that went "...tears get in your powdered wrinkles, when the son goes away so does the world," and other such songs. Just as the ten most popular songs these days are all about tender feelings between men and women, the most popular songs in those days were about love between mothers and sons—not blessed or ordinary ones, but mothers and sons who were sad or had been torn away from each other. The mother-child bonds were the earliest bonds in a person's life and often the deepest, so it was nearly beastly. Misfortune was especially beastly. They could not be tamed by culture, artificiality, tradition, or custom, and so returned to nature, the forest, primitiveness, and nakedness.

Would that there were twelve acts, or even five acts of *pansori* then! *Yukchabaegi*, half sighing and half singing, lived on feebly through the beats tapped out with pokers and canes.[3] The *nongak* band that went from house to house on the Lunar New Year to banish demons and mischievous spir-

오래되었다. 깝데기를 벳기냐? 벗고 싶고, 벗을 수 있다고 믿고, 벗었다고 생각하면, 벗은 것이나 다름없었다. 옷을 입고 있으면서 벗은 것이나 다름없으면, 벗은 것보다 더 나빴다. 벗었으니 해롭고, 입은 옷이 소용없으니 헤프고, 제 것 소중한 줄 모르니 헛되고, 두고 근천을 떠니 흉했다. 소수 양반들이 잘 먹고 잘 살았던 왕조 때도 나라를 젊어진 것은 많은 상놈들이었지만, 나라가 망한 다음에도 명줄을 이은 것은 역시 그들이었다. 그들이 망한 나라를 버티는 것은 나라를 말아먹은 놈들이 나라가 망한 다음에도 잘 먹고 잘 사는 것처럼 당연했다. 종들인 그들이 주인이었다. 풀린 사람들을 해방한다는 놈도 미친놈이고, 갇힌 사람들을 해방됐다고 하는 놈도 제정신이 아니었다. 사람들은 풀리기도 하고 갇히기도 했다. 같은 사람이 열리기도 하고 또 닫히기도 했다. 배운 놈은 설명해서 유식했고, 못 배운 놈은 몰라서 무식했다. 세상은 설명이 잘 안 되었다. 무식한 놈이 옳았다. 그는 적어도 억지를 쓰지 않았다. 모른 것이 하도 많아서, 알아봤자 별수 없었고, 몰라봤자 별것 아니었다. 안 것이 많을수록 모른 것이 많았고, 무식했다. 그는 그날 밤, 감을 따러 부모 몰래 담장께로 갔다. 아버지는

its, the shrine tree at every village entrance that wore different clothes every season and stood like a hermit as it protected the peace of the village, and the shrine *kut* that took place there were considered totem poles and shaman rituals that belonged to an ignorant people that still believed in barbaric superstitions. Thanks to the thirty some years of relentless cultivation by the island people who had opened their harbors early and accepted Western culture, most things of the past were wrecked. The parts that survived lived wretched but resilient lives among the baser class. The mean subsisted on the stale and less spoiled. Not only did this class live on, but it grew as those from above continued to sink lower and lower. The noblemen who hastened to abandon the old were suspended in the air. In spite of the careful and unabating work of the dwarves, the transition between the old and the new in the land of savages was not yet complete. The new had not reached the lower class or taken root in the upper class. The result was a cultural void. Films and cars were new, but theatre and dance, music and art, folkore and legends, and even literature and history were thrown out before the new could even arrive to

피신 중이었고, 어머니는 건넌방에서 소설책을 읽었다.

"누구야!"

그가 혹시 어디서 눈먼 총알이 날아올까 봐 허리를 납작 굽히고 쥐새끼처럼 살금살금 감나무 몸통에 기어 올라 막 첫가지에 한쪽 다리를 걸치고 감에 한 팔을 뻗쳤을 때, 시커먼 그림자 하나가 담을 넘어 담 위에 납작 엎드리더니, 그가 미처 뭐라고 하기 전에 담 밑으로 툭 떨어졌다. 괴물의 머리가 거의 그의 발끝에 닿았다. 그것이 사방을 두리번거렸다. 그가 꽥을 질렀지만, 그의 목구멍을 기어 나온 것은 모기소리였다. 괴한이 깜짝 놀라 담벽에 찰싹 달라붙었다.

"쉬, 쉬잇."

"도, 도둑!"

그가 발을 헛딛고 땅바닥에 떨어졌다. 두 사람들의 얼굴이 거의 맞닿았다.

"나, 나여."

"나라니, 누구?"

"보면 몰르냐?"

"이 새끼. 감 도독놈."

"지가 김시롱."

replace them. "In with the new" had been confused with "Out with the old." They had hastily incinerated the ancestral tablets which they replaced with insubstantial fakes. The misguided enthusiasm for borrowed, donated, scavenged clothes over one's own, and the stripping of one's own clothes to wear the clothes of others were a mistake. Changing clothes itself was not a mistake, but believing that they could change clothes, that no trouble would come of it, that it would make life rather much easier—that was a mistake.

In culture, destruction is possible only through creation. One should not indiscriminately wear someone else's clothes or take off one's own. Even if the clothes are nothing but rags, throwing away one's clothes without having something to change into is insane. But what is more insane is the belief that one should change into new clothes just because they no longer like their rags. Even if they believed they were wearing rags, they were not. Not all things old are rags. Skin is old. Should we peel that off, too? If they wanted to take it off, if they believed and thought they had shed it, they were as good as undressed. If they wore clothes but were as good as undressed, it was worse than

"나는 우리 집 감인디."

"옆집 감 좀 따묵으면 안 되냐?"

"참말로 감 따묵을라고 왔냐? 뭔 놈의 배창시가 난리도 몰르냐?"

"니는? 니 배창시도 염치가 없다."

"얼렁 둬 개 따갖고 가."

"아니여. 느그 집 옆집 감 좀 따자."

"새끼. 그 집 감은 떫어."

"떫은 감이 맛있어, 곶감 깎으면."

"니 감 따묵을라고 온 것 아니지?"

"그래. 용완이 성, 집에 있을까?"

"난리통에 어디를 돌아다니냐, 집에 있지?"

"아니다. 빨갱이들이 시를 접수했는디 집에 들어백혀 있겠냐?"

"접수허다니, 시가 무슨 서류냐?"

"조용히 해. 니도 같이 가자. 용완이 성헌테 부탁이 있어."

"무슨 부탁? 숙제? 니가 해. 나도 산술 모른 것이 하나 있는디."

"우리 아부지 목숨을 부탁해야 돼. 인자 빨갱이 세상이라더라. 안 들어주면 이 칼로 죽여뿔란다."

being stark naked. It was hazardous because they were undressed, wasteful because their clothes did no good, meaningless because they did not value what was their own, and distasteful because they griped about all of it. Under a monarchy where a small minority of noblemen are well fed and clothed, it is the vast majority of the lower class that bear the weight of the country, and it is the lower class who survive when the country falls.

The fact that the lower class continued to bear the weight of the fallen nation was as unsurprising as the continuing wealth of the upper class, whether they had sovereignty or not. The slaves were the masters. The fools tried to liberate the free, while lunatics insisted that the captive had been liberated. People were freed and captured. The same person could be open-minded or narrow-minded. The educated were intelligent because they lectured and explained, and the uneducated were ignorant because they did not know. The world eluded explanation. The ignorant were right. At least they did not make outrageous claims. There was so much they did not know that it did them no good to know, and what they did not know did not matter anyway. The more they knew,

그가 참말로 주머니에서 주머니칼을 꺼내 날을 펴 보였다.

"느그 아부지가 시키든?"

"우리 아부지는 도망쳤어."

"참말로 죽여뿔래?"

"야, 가시내 같은 용완이 성 하나 못 죽이냐?"

"맞어, 나도 죽이겠다. 키도 우리허고 같어."

"니허고 같지. 나보다는 작어."

"공부 잘하면 등치가 작냐? 씨름허면 내가 이긴다."

용완이 성은 그들보다 서너 살 위였다. 그는 아마 보통학교 때 월반을 해서 중학교 사학년이었다. 중학 사년이면 거짓말이 아니라 그들만한 아들을 둔 액압씨가 있었다. 그는 전교에서 아무도 따라가지 못하는 일등짜리 천재였다. 이상하게도 그가 그들보다 공부를 더 열심히 했다. 열심해서 잘한다면 이상할 것도 없었지만, 그는 해도 너무 열심이었다. 아마 할수록 할 것이 더 생기는 모양이었다. 그는 잠자는 시간 말고는 전부 책과 씨름이었다. 먹으면서는 물론, 놀면서도 책을 읽었다. 그는 아예 놀지를 않았지만, 그들이 놀러 가면 한 번도 바쁘다고 핑계대지 않고 언제든지 같이 놀아주었다. 그

the more they did not know, and so they were all ignorant.

That night, the boy snuck out of the house and crept towards the wall to pick persimmons. His father had gone in hiding, and his mother was reading a novel in the other room.

"Who is it?"

Afraid of stray bullets, the boy hunkered down as he snuck over to the tree and climbed it as quietly as a mouse. He had just swung his leg over the lowest branch and was reaching for a persimmon when he saw a dark shadow hop onto the wall, lie flat on top of it, and fall to the base of the wall before the boy could say anything. The monster's head grazed the boy's foot. He looked around. He screamed—but the only thing that escaped his throat was a mosquito buzz. The intruder, startled, stood flat against the wall.

"Shhh!"

"Thief! Thief!"

The boy's foot slipped and he fell to the ground. Their faces nearly touched.

"It's me."

"Who's 'me?'"

"Don't you recognize me?"

에게는 좋아하는 경기가 없었다. 무엇이든 그들이 하자는 대로 했다.

모르면 배워가면서 했다. 차례를 기다리는 동안 그는 책을 읽었다. 독받기를 하다가도 돌을 떨어뜨려 죽으면 그는 즉시 책을 집어 들었다. 적이 돌을 떨어뜨리는지, 돌을 받으면 몇 동우를 받는지, 다섯을 다 받는지 하나도 못 받는지, 그는 관심이 없는 것 같았다. 승벽이 없어서 지나 이기나 똑같은 그와 경쟁을 하는 것이 싱겁고 재미가 없을 것 같았지만, 그렇지 않았다. 그는 차례가 되면 금방 그들하고 똑같이 기승을 부리고 낄낄대며 즐겁게 놀았다. 중학생이, 그것도 사학년이 소학생하고 독받기를 하는 것부터가 예삿일이 아니었다. 그가 그들과 똑같이 노는 것만으로 충분히 그들은 열광했다. 놀때 그는 그들보다 더 어렸다. 아무도 그가 틈틈이 책을 펼쳐드는 것을 시비하지 않았다. 책을 보는 것은 중학사년이었고, 독받기를 하는 것은 소학생이었다. 그 둘이 한 사람에게서 만나자 팽팽한 긴장이 생겼다. 그 긴장에 그들은 흥분했다.

"성 헐 차례야."

"벌써 돌아왔냐? 왜 그렇게 빨리 온다냐?"

"You persimmon thief."

"You should talk."

"These persimmons belong to our house."

"We're neighbors. Share your persimmons."

"Are you really here for the persimmons? You've got some balls. Don't you know we're in the middle of a war?"

"What about you? Your balls have no conscience."

"Take a couple and go. Quick!"

"Nah, let's get some from your neighbors' tree."

"Their persimmons are still bitter, stupid."

"Bitter persimmons are good. You can dry them."

"You're not here for the persimmons, are you?"

"No. Do you think Yong-wan's at home?"

"He won't be out wandering during a war."

"No. The reds have appropriated the city. He's not going to stay hidden at home."

"What do you mean 'appropriated?' What's appropriate about taking over?"

"Quiet. You should come with me. I need to ask Yong-wan for a favor."

"What favor? Homework? Do it yourself. I have one math question I can't solve, but I'm not asking anyone for help."

"I have to ask him to save my father's life. I hear

"세 짜가리야."

"그래? 두 짜가린 줄 알았다."

"그렇더라도 그렇지. 왜 한 짜가리부터 해?"

"내가 한 짜가리부터 했냐?"

"독을 한 개씩 집어먹었으니 한 짜가리지."

"내가 하나씩 먹었냐?"

"하나씩 먹었는지 두 개씩 먹었는지 몰라?"

"맞어. 두 개씩 집었다."

"아니, 한 개씩."

"그래, 한 개씩. 그럼 죽나?"

"세 짜가리 하다가 돌을 하나고 둘이고 떨어뜨리면 안 죽어?"

"지금은 안 움직였다. 가만 놔뒀다. 그래도 죽냐?"

성은 놀 때 보면 어린애 같다 못해서 바보 같았다. 그들에게도 쩔쩔맸다. 놀이를 못해서도 그들에게 졌지만, 놀이의 규칙이나 진행 방법을 가지고도 그들에게 꼼짝 못했다. 그들이 대체로 옳았지만, 더러 그가 옳고 그들이 틀렸을 때도 그들이 우기면 그가 졌다. 아마 뜻이 콩밭에 있어서 그랬겠지만, 그들은 그것이 그가 생김새처럼 마음씨도 가날퍼서 그랬다고 생각했다. 그는 공부만

62

it's the reds' world now. If he turns me down, I'm going to kill him with this knife."

He pulled out a pocket knife and opened it.

"Did your father put you up to this?"

"My father ran away."

"Are you really going to kill him?"

"Yong-wan's like a girl. You don't think I can take him?"

"True. I could take him, too. He's the same height as us."

"He's the same height as you. He's shorter than me."

"Do you think smart people are usually smaller? I can beat him at wrestling."

Yong-wan was three or four years their senior. He skipped a grade in primary school and was now in the fourth year of secondary school. In those days, a boy in the fourth year of secondary school could have a son, like kid's pop did. Yong-wan was the top of his class, a genius no one could beat. So it was odd that he studied much harder than the other boys. There was nothing strange about his hard work yielding good results, but he worked too hard. Perhaps the more he studied the more he discovered new things to study. He wrestled with

아니면 그들의 동무가 되기에도 부족했다.

"니 칼 있냐? 단도면 더욱 좋고, 식칼도 괜찮고, 안 되면 연필칼도 할 수 없다."

"감이나 묵고, 우리 집에서 놀다 가거라."

"과도!"

"정제칼로 깎아 묵는다. 그냥 엉덩이에 씩씩 문대서 껍질째 묵기도 허고."

"니는 집 봐라. 어려울 때 부모를 안 돌보면 언제 돌보냐?"

"참말로 갈래? 칼 필요 없다. 몽둥이면 충분하다. 몽둥이도 소양없다. 그 성 니 칼만 봐도 기절한다."

"그래. 니는 따라만 와. 안 따라와도 좋고."

"안 따라가면 길만 빌리냐? 임진왜란 같다. 풍신수길이가 명나라 친다고 조선한테 길을 빌렸단 말이다."

"나 풍신수길 안 헐란다. 내가 왜 풍신이야? 내가 왜 푼수냐?"

"제발 허지 마라. 수길이도 명나라까지 못 갔다."

"그것 봐라. 나는 간다."

그들은 몸을 낮추고 그의 집 마당을 가로질러 옆집 담을 차례로 넘었다. 용완이 성은 누나와 함께 그 집 방

books every waking moment. He read as he ate, and even as he played. He did not play at all, but when the boys went over to play with him, he always obliged them. He did not have a sport he liked. He played whatever game they picked. If he didn't know the game, he learned as he played. He read in between turns. When he played *tokbadki,* he picked up his book the second he dropped his pebble.[4] He didn't seem to care if his opponent dropped his pebble, how many pebbles he caught, if all five were caught, or none at all. One might think that his friends got bored playing with him because of his lack of a competitive drive and because he did not care if he won or lost, but this was not the case. When his turn came around, he played enthusiastically, struggling and laughing like the others. It was unusual for a secondary school kid—a fourth-year, no less—to play *tokbadki* with primary school children. Just the fact that Yong-wan played with the boys made them crazy about him. When he played with the boys, he became more of a child than the boys. No one objected to his reading while he played. Yong-wan was a secondary school fourth-year when he read, and a primary school kid when he played *tokbadki*. The

한 칸을 세 들어 살았다. 그들은 날쌔게 그 방 앞으로 가서 마루 밑에 엎드렸다. 그들이 자주 와서 놀았던 마루였다. 그들은 방보다 마루나 마당에서 놀았다. 방은 그의 누나 차지였다. 그의 누나는 그들이 갈 때마다 방에서 바느질을 했다. 그와 그의 누나는 가난했다. 그의 누나는 그나 그들보다 십 년은 더 늙은 부인이었는데, 그들은 그녀의 남편을 본 적이 없었다. 그 방은 불이 꺼지고 인기척이 없었다. 그들이 막 용완이 성을 부르려 했을 때 등 뒤에서 가래 돋구는 소리가 났다. 그것은 틀림없이 그 집 주인 영감이었다.

"웬 놈들이냐? 용완이는 아침에 나가서 안직 안 들어왔다."

"용완이 성 누님은요?" 그가 배짱 좋게 허리를 펴고 물었다.

"뭣이여?" 늙은 우샌이 그를 물끄러미 쳐다보았다. 그가 얼른 허리를 굽히고 굽신 절을 했다. "오냐. 니가 뉘 집 아들네미냐? 정샌떡은 금방 요 앞에 어디 나간갑더라."

노인은 험, 험, 헛기침을 하면서 큰방 쪽으로 사라졌고, 그들은 마루 끝에 걸터앉았다. 그는 용완이 성이 그들과 꼰을 두다가 비번이 되어 잠간 책에 눈 붙이러 방

two personalities in one person created great tension. This tension excited the boys.

"It's your turn, Yong-wan."

"So soon? That was quick."

"You're on three pebbles."

"Really? I thought I was on two pebbles."

"So why did you start at one pebble?"

"I started at one pebble?"

"You only picked up one pebble at a time, so that's starting at one pebble."

"I picked up one pebble at a time?"

"You don't remember how many pebbles you picked up?"

"I thought I picked up two at a time."

"No, it was one."

"Right. One. So my turn's over?"

"If you drop two when you're suppose to be on three pebbles, aren't you out?"

"I didn't drop any this time. Am I still out?"

When Yong-wan played, he was so childlike that he appeared soft in the head. The boys were no match for him. He lost because he was bad at the games, but he also could not keep track of the rules. They were usually right, but when Yong-wan was right, they would argue until he admitted de-

에 들어간 것 같은 기분이 들었다. 그들이 부르면, 금방이라도 그가, 또 그의 차례가 됐냐, 하고, 가시내처럼, 바보처럼, 헤헤 웃으면서 마루로 나올 것 같았다. 아니, 혹시 난리통에 죽었을까? 집에서 공부나 하지 않고 돌아다니다가 유탄에 맞아 죽어버린 것 아닐까? 그는 그의 방정맞은 생각을 털어버리려고 머리를 흔들었다. 그가 그때, 그가 죽기는 왜 죽어? 하는 듯이 보통 때처럼 터덜터덜 나타나면 얼마나 좋을까. 그는 몸을 떨었다. 그가 연필칼이고 정제칼이고 몸에 지니지 않은 것은 참 잘했다.

"춥냐?"

"니 칼 버려. 나한테 맡기든지."

"칼이 없으면 뭘로 찌르냐? 손가락으로 찌르냐?"

"용완이 성은 니 부탁 들어준다. 안 들어주면 들어줄 힘이 없다."

"그것 쓸 일 없어서 좋겠다."

"쓸데없는 것을 왜 가지고 있냐?"

"있는지 없는지 알아볼라고."

"가지고 있으면 쓸 일이 생기고, 없으면 안 생긴다."

"누가 정신병자냐, 있는 대로 써뿔게?"

feat. Yong-wan was distracted, but the boys thought that Yong-wan lost because his temperament was as frail as his appearance. If it wasn't for his smarts, he would have been too frail even to be their friend.

"Do you have a knife? A dagger? A kitchen knife is good. If not, pencil knife works, too."

"Have a persimmon, hang out at our house, and go home."

"Or a paring knife!"

"We don't have a paring knife. We use the kitchen knife to peel fruit. Or we just wipe the fruit on the butts of our pants and eat it, peel and all."

"You stay at home. You should look after your parents during a difficult time."

"Are you really going? You don't need a knife. You can bring a club. You don't even need a club. Yong-wan will faint the second he sees your knife."

"Okay. Why don't you just come along then? Or not. I don't care."

"So you're just asking to pass through? It's like the the Imjin War. Toyotomi Hideyoshi asked for passage through Joseon to attack Ming."

"I don't want to be Hideyoshi. Why am I Hideyo-

"그래. 느그 외삼촌. 느그 아부지헌테 쌀 떨어졌다고 돈 빌려갖고 집에 가다가 술집 앞을 지나면서 술 냄새가 솔솔 나면 집 쌀독에 거미줄 슨 것을 깜빡 잊어버리는 느그 외삼촌."

"니는 넘의 집 일을 느그 집 일겉이 왜 그렇게 자상하게 아냐?"

"니가 다 얘기했다. 여러 번."

"내가 내 외삼촌이냐? 외삼촌이 정신없다고 조카도 정신이 나가냐? 참말! 우리 외삼촌도."

"사람은 외가 쪽을 많이 탁한다더라. 모성이 우성이라더라."

"느그 집에는 외가 쪽으로 빨갱이 없냐?"

"느그 외삼촌도 빨갱이냐?"

"울 아부지가 처남은 정신 나갔다고 했어. 그 말이 미쳤다는 말이고 미쳤다는 말이 빨갱이란 말이지 뭐."

"저기 빨갱이 하나 온다."

"뭐? 우리 외삼촌?"

용완이 성이 웬 낯선 남자하고 들어왔다. 그들을 보고 그는 놀랐지만 곧 반색을 했다.

"돌차기 허로 왔냐?"

shi? I'm not hideous."

"Don't please Sugil didn't reach Ming."

"See? I'm coming."

They crept across his yard and climbed over the wall to the next house. Yong-wan and his sister had rented one of the rooms in that house. The boys dashed over to Yong-wan's room and crawled under the porch. They often played on that porch. The room was his sister's space. When Yong-wan came out to play with them, his sister sewed in the room. He and his sister were poor. His sister was ten years older than Yong-wan, but she had never had a husband. The light was out in the room and no sound came from inside. They were about to call him when someone hawked some spittle loudly behind them. It was no doubt the old man, the owner of the house.

"What are you kids doing here? Yong-wan went out this morning and hasn't returned."

"What about his sister?" The boy got to his feet and spoke fearlessly.

"What did you say to me?" Mr. old Wu stared at the boy, who quickly bowed to the old man a few times. "That's more like it. Whose son are you? The wife of Mr. Jeong went out for a quick visit nearby."

"밤중에?"

"왜, 금이 안 보이냐? 공부허로 왔냐? 숙제 있냐?"

"야들은 누구요?"

"동네 아이들이오."

"심부름 시킬 수 있소? 믿을 수 있소?"

"믿을 수는 있지만 너무 어리지요."

"그 말이 그 말이오. 어려서 힘을 못 쓰니 믿을 수 없소."

"힘만 세면 아무나 믿소?"

"우리는요 힘 쎄요." 그의 친구가 끼여들었다.

"믿지는 마." 그가 덧붙였다. "우리는 성 편이 아니야."

"한편이 아니면 적이냐?" 용완이 성 친구가 받았다.
"적이면 싸울래?"

낯선 사람이 그의 목덜미를 거머잡았다. 그가 빠져나
오려고 버둥댔지만, 발들이 땅 위로 떴다. 그는 숨이 막
혔다. 겁이 나거나 무서운 대신에, 화가 나고 창피했다.
얼굴이 붉어지고, 눈알이 튀어나오고, 눈물이 났다. 그
는 무력했다. 픽, 소리가 났다. 어른이 억, 하고 그를 놓
아주었다. 그의 친구가 쥐새끼처럼 날쎄게 어둠 속으로
달아났다. 그가 마침내 일을 낸 모양이었다.

"저놈, 저놈 잡아."

The old man cleared his throat loudly as he retreated into the main room. They sat on the edge
of the porch. It was as though the three of them
were playing a board game together and Yong-
wan was sitting out one game to read in his room.
If they called him right now, he would come out to
the porch giggling like a girl, like an idiot, Is it my
turn already? Or perhaps he had died in the war?
He'd been hit by a stray bullet while out wandering
instead of studying at home? He shook his head to
shake off the unfortunate thoughts. How he wished
Yong-wan would appear right that moment and
say, Die? Never! He shivered. It was a good thing
he did not have any knives on him, pencil knives or
kitchen knives.

"Are you cold?"

"You should toss your knife. Or I can hold onto it
for you."

"What am I going to stab Yong-wan with if I don't
have a knife? My finger?"

"Yong-wan will do what you ask him to do. Even
if he doesn't it'll be because he's weak."

"Good thing I won't need to use the knife."

"So why are you carrying around something you
don't need?"

"어른이 아들을 데리고 난리요?"

"어른, 아가 어디 있소, 박치기에?" 어른이 턱쪼가리를 손으로 어루만지고 말했다.

"딴 디는 성허요?" 그가 주먹으로 눈물을 닦으면서 말했다. "나는 칼인 줄 알았소."

사내가 또 발끈해서 그에게 달려들었다. 도망간 놈 쫓느니, 옆에서 이죽거리는 놈 요절낼 요량이었다. 독이 오른 그가 꿈쩍 않고 버티자, 사내가 턱뼈 바스러진 것을 두 손바닥들로 이리저리 맞추는 시늉을 했다. 용완이 성이 얼른 그들 사이로 끼여들었다. 그는 몸으로 그를 감싸고 입으로 그를 나무랐다.

"니 시방 장난인 줄 아냐? 칼이 노리개냐? 농담으로 찔러도 참말로 죽어, 피가 나오고."

"용완이 성도. 시방 누구 부지깽이 갖고 골목대장 허요? 칼이 진짠디, 피가 가짜요?"

"니는 왜 겁이 없냐? 칼이야 흔치. 흔타고 아무나 휘두르냐?"

"성도. 친구 숨통이 끊어지는디 안 휘두르면 언제 휘두르요? 죽은 뒤 뫼뚱 앞에 가서 무당 칼춤 추요, 초혼가 부름서?"

"Because I might need it."

"If you have it on you, you'll use it. If you don't, you won't."

"I'm not crazy. I won't use it if I don't have to."

"Right. What about your uncle on your mother's side? The one who borrows money from your father and always tells him he's out of rice. The one who smells liquor while passing a pub on the way home and forgets about the empty rice jar."

"How do you know about other people's family matters like they're your own?"

"Because you told me. Several times."

"I'm not my uncle! Just because the uncle is an idiot, doesn't mean the nephew is also an idiot. Really! My uncle is too stupid!"

"I hear people take after relatives from their mother's side. The mother's side is dominant."

"You don't have reds on your mother's side?"

"Your uncle is a red."

"My dad said, 'My brother-in-law is out of his mind.' That means he's crazy. And if you're crazy, you're a red."

"Here comes a red."

"Who, my uncle?"

Just then Yong-wan walked in with a stranger.

"쬐깐헌 것이 똘것이네?" 낯선 사내가 마무리하듯 턱을 톡톡 두드리고 말했다.

"턱이 덜 떨어졌소?"

"저 새끼, 칵 볿아 쥑여뿔라."

"어른헌테 함부로 말하면 되냐?"

"어른도." 그가 지지 않고 받았다. "전시라 노소간에 신경들이 날카로운갑소."

"니, 집에 가거라. 나중에 놀자. 지금은 놀 때가 아니다."

"누가 놀로 온 줄 알어?"

"볼일이 있어 왔냐?"

"봉수가 성헌테 부탁이 있다요."

"무슨 일인디?"

"즈그 아부지 목숨."

"봉수 아부지가 누군디?"

"옆집 삼서 그것도 몰라?"

"안다. 즈그 외삼촌도 알고."

"그럼 다 아네. 나는 오늘사 알았는디."

"니는 몰라도 된다."

"모른다고 총알이 비껴가? 방금 안 봤어? 숨통이 막혀서 쎄바닥 빼물고 죽었어, 박치기 아니면."

Yong-wan was surprised to see them but greeted them happily.

"Are you here to play hopscotch?"

"In the middle of the night?" asked the stranger.

"Why not? Can't you see the lines? Are you here to study? Do you have homework?"

"Who are these kids?"

"They're from the village."

"Can they run errands? Can they be trusted?"

"They can be trusted, but they're too young."

"Then they can't be trusted. They're too weak to be trusted."

"And you can trust anyone who's strong?"

"We're strong," the boy's friend interrupted.

"But don't trust us," said the boy. "We're not on your side, Yong-wan."

"If you're not on our side, are you the enemy?" demanded the stranger. "You wanna fight?"

The stranger seized him by the collar. The boy's friend struggled to free himself, but his feet dangled in the air. He couldn't breathe. He wasn't afraid, but he was angry, and embarrassed. His face turned red, his eyes bulged, and tears slid down his cheeks. He was helpless.

Suddenly there was a loud sound. Wham! Oof,

"병수 아부지는 시방 어디 있냐?"

"벌써 죽었을랑가 몰라. 병수가 아니라 봉수."

"아직 안 죽었으면 곧 죽어."

"그런 말은 아무라도 할 수 있어. 누구는 곧 안 죽어?"

"곧이 길다. 내 곧은 짧다. 니 곧은 길고 길었으면 좋겠다. 길 사람 곧이 짧아도 볼썽사납고, 짧을 사람 곧이 길어도 볼꼴 안 좋다."

"볼꼴 보고 세상 살어?"

"그랬으면 얼마나 좋겠냐? 집에 가거라. 모양새가 좋을라고 또 만날지 모르겠다."

"반란군이 쳐들어와 좋은 세상 되았는디?"

"해방구는 좋다마는 바깥반동 준동한다. 무한송전 좋아 마라 진압군이 진격한다."

"세상이 또 뒤집히냐?"

"니는 딴것 걱정 말고 심국지나 더 읽어라. 생제갈이 칠성단에 동남풍을 비는구나. 사제갈이 주생중달, 우선 들고 우화등선. 범수 놈도 집 바깥을 한 발짝도 못 나가리."

"범수가 아니라 봉수."

"봉수냐. 횃불이 타지도 못하고 꺼졌다. 입성이 곧 퇴각이라, 뜻을 펴긴 고사하고 잘난 체할 틈도 없다. 우리는

78

said the man Yong-wan had come with and let go.
The boy's friend disappeared in to the dark, quick
as a mouse. The boy had really done it this time.

"Get him! Get him!"

"What's a grown man doing picking on babies?"

"There are no grown men or babies when it
comes to head-butting," he said, rubbing his jaw.

"Did he hurt you anywhere else?" the boy asked,
wiping his tears with his fist. "I thought he used the
knife on you."

The man charged at the boy again. It was better
to finish off the one who remained and teased him
rather than to chase the one who got away. When
the boy spitefully stood his ground, the man
rubbed his jaw with both hands, as if to put the
broken pieces of his jaw back into place. Yong-
wan quickly stepped in between them. He wrapped
the boy in his arms and led him aside.

"You think this is a game?" Yong-wan quietly
chided. "You think that knife is a toy? If you stab
someone as a joke, he'll really bleed. Even die."

"You think I'm horsing around? Trying to look
tough in the neighborhood? This knife is real. This
blood is real."

"Why aren't you afraid? Yes, there are plenty of

도망갈 준비를 서둔다. 느그는 며칠만 조용히 참아라."

"성이 왜 도망가?"

"본색이 들통이 났는디."

용완이 성의 마지막이었다. 그의 누이가 황급히 들어오고, 낯선 남자들 몇이 그 뒤를 따랐다. 그들은 그가 거기 있는 것 따위는 아랑곳하지 않고 보따리 싸고 산으로 달아날 궁리를 했다. 입성하자 퇴각이라니, 원래 성을 점령하면 합법적이고 정당한 개선 말고도, 온갖 불법적이고 야비하고 포악한 약탈과 유린이 자행되는 법 아닌가. 그것이 왜 패잔병 줄행랑이냐? 왜군이 동래에서 도망길 찾았냐, 머나먼 의주길 놔두고? 승리에 취해서 정신을 버리고 길길이 날뛰는 무리들 속에서 쥐구멍 찾자고 엉뚱한 소리를 한다면 현자가 미쳤다. 승리의 한가운데에서 그것이 헛된 것이라고 생떼를 쓰다니! 그것이 덧없는 줄 누가 모르냐. 애당초 그것을 탐내면 틀렸다. 현명한 사람은 처음에 싸움을 말렸다. 그날 밤 용완이 성의 모습이 그의 머리에서 얼른 지워지지 않았다. 그는 삼국지 대신, 읽던 탐정소설을 마저 읽었다. 그가 마지막 쪽을 읽고 책을 덮었을 때 마루의 벽시계가 열두 점을 쳤다. 그때 천장에서 작은 돌멩이나 흙덩이

knives, but that doesn't mean anyone should go around wielding them."

"When's a better time to swing a knife than when your friend's getting strangled? At his grave? When you're doing the knife dance like a shaman? In the middle of a dirge?"

"That little thing's sure got a mouth on him!" The stranger remarked, tapping his chin as though he had finished putting his jaw back together.

"Need another kick in your trap?"

"I'm going to stamp the light out of the little shit!"

"That's no way to talk to an adult."

"Adults too. People are snipping, old or young, because of war."

"You. Go home. We'll play later. This is no time for games."

"You think I'm here to play?"

"Then why are you here?"

"Bong-su needed a favor from you."

"What?"

"His father's life."

"Who's Bong-su's father?"

"You don't know his father? You're neighbors!"

"I know. I know his uncle, too."

"So you know all of them. I only found out about

하나가 떨어지는 소리가 팽팽한 종이 위로 쨍, 하고 났다. 크지 않은 소리였지만, 한밤중이라 간이 떨어지게 큰 소리로 들렸다. 그것이 그 사흘의 첫날 밤의 가장 놀라운 사건이라면 사건이었다.

이튿날, 학교를 가지 못하는 것 말고는 별일이 없었다. 그에게는 금족령이 내려졌다. 바깥도 조용했다. 전날 총소리에 비하면 평화로운 것이 신기했다. 잔적 소탕도 없었고, 개선 행진도 없었다. 검거도 동원도 없었다. 겉으로는 달라진 것이 없었다. 그는 어른들의 눈치를 살폈다. 그들도 깜깜하기로는 마찬가지였다. 더러 그들 중에는 큰길가까지 진출한 사람이 있었지만, 대개 골목 안 정보였다.

"북진 통일이 됐다요." 물을 길은 동네 아주머니가 물동이를 장독대 담에 올려놓고 동이 밑으로 흐르는 물을 손바닥으로 닦으며 말했다.

"북진 통일이? 이 박사가 밀고 올라갔는가?" 그의 어머니가 반쯤 닳아진 동강 숟갈로 붉은 고구마 껍질을 긁다 말고 고개를 쳐들었다.

"쳐내려왔지 어찌 밀고 올라갔다요?" 쭈그리고 앉아서 빨래를 하고 있던 또 한 아주머니가 끼여들었다. "공

them today."

"It's none of your business."

"Can I run through bullets without getting hurt if it's none of my business? Didn't you see what just happened? He would have choked to death with his tongue sticking out if it wasn't for that head-butt."

"Where's Byeong-su's father now?"

"He might be dead already. And it's Bong-su, not Byeong-su."

"If he's not dead already, he will be soon."

"You could say that about anyone. Everyone could die soon."

"For some people, 'soon' is later. My 'soon' will come sooner than yours. I hope your 'soon' is much, much later. It's awful if a person's 'soon' is sooner than it should be, and it's unsightly if it's later than it should be."

"You live life for it to be pretty?"

"If only that were true! Go home. If life is pretty, we'll meet again."

"The rebel forces have arrived and the world will be better, won't it?"

"Hurrah for the liberated region, but the reactionaries are stirring. No time to rejoice in the un-

산당들이 밀고 내려와서 이겼다요."

"밀고 내려와? 그럼 남진 통일이그만?"

"아, 북쪽에서 쳐들어왔는디 어찌 남진이다요, 북진이지?"

"북벌남정 좌충우돌 오매불망 쌈질인가?"

"군인들이 밀고 내려왔다요?" 표모가 조심스럽게 추측했다.

"맞소, 군대가 밀어붙였다요. 병정들 아니면 누가 쳐들어온다요?" 물 긷는 아주머니는 좀 더 자신이 있었다.

"같은 군인들인디." 표모는 미심쩍었다.

"군인들이 화가 나서 순사들을 요절냈쟈." 집주인 아주머니가 결론을 내렸다.

"어찌 한솥에 밥을 먹음서 싸워싼다요? 싸우면 즈그들이나 싸우지 왜 애맨 사람들 분탕질이다요?"

"삼팔선이 터져서 통일이 됐당께요. 안 그러면 어떻게 압록강에서 전기가 여기까지 온다요? 엊저녁에 밤새도록 불이 안 들어옵디여?" 북진파 아주머니가 사실을 증거 삼아 주장했다.

"특선 쓰는 집도 인자 재미 다 봤는갑소. 다 특선인디? 시도 때도 없이 불 들어오면 그것이 특선 아니요?" 표모가 부화뇌동했다.

limited electricity supply—the foe is advancing."

"The world is turning upside-down again?"

"Don't worry about a thing and keep reading *Romance of the Three Kingdoms*. The live Zhuge prays for a southeasterly wind at the Seven Star Stand. The dead Zhuge makes the living Zhongda flee. With a feather fan in hand, ascend to the heavens and become a hermit. Beom-su won't be able to take a step outside his house."[5]

"It's Bong-su, not Beom-su."

"Bong-su is his name? The flames were extinguished before they could burn.[6] We retreat as soon as we conquer the castle—there is no time to gloat, let alone carry out our ideals. We must prepare to flee. You boys lay low for a few days."

"Why are you running away?"

"My cover's been blown."

That was the last of Yong-wan. His sister rushed in with a few men. No one paid any attention to the boy as they hurriedly packed their things to escape into the mountains. Retreating the moment they conquered. Conquering the castle meant all kinds of illegal, egregious, and violent actions and violations were about to take place along with a number of legal and rightful changes. So why were they

"그동안 쓴 것만도 어딘디? 호롱불에 밥을 묵으면 밥이 입으로 들어가는지 코로 들어가는지 몰라 정신이 통 없어. 끄시름은 또 어쩌고. 등잔만 안 봐도 살겄어."

"불을 끄고 묵어도 밥알이 설마 코로 들어갈라고. 하로 이틀 밥 묵었어?"

"허기는 밥이 없어 못 묵지, 어두워서 못 묵을랍디요." 표모의 말은 온건한 것인지, 한술 더 뜨는 것인지, 분명치 않았다.

"캄캄헌 디서 먹통 밥을 묵다가, 훤헌 디서 대낮 밥을 묵응께, 먹통 밥 묵기가 얼마나 사나웠는가 새삼스럽더란 말이요."

"밥이야 덜 볿아도 묵지만, 아들 공부야 글씨가 가물가물해서, 허다못해 남폿불이라도 있어야지, 촛불은 못 사줘도."

"인자 촛불 백 개보다 더 볿은 디서 공부도 허고 밥도 묵게 되았소."

"옛날에는 불이 잘 안 들어오고, 와도 천장에다가 홍시 하나 걸어놓은 것만 했는디."

"남쪽은 전기가 모자라고 북쪽은 남아돈다요."

"남은 전기 뭣 헌다요? 밥 비베 묵는다요?"

retreating like they were the defeated troops? Like Japanese troops escaping via the faraway Uiju instead of Dongnae during the Imjin War? The sage is crazy if he's looking for holes to hide in the midst of crowds that are drunk and wild with victory. How dare he argue in the middle of the victory celebrations that was all for naught? Everyone knows it was all for naught. It was wrong to covet the conquest in the first place. The sage had been against the fight from the start.

The boy would not easily forget his last moments with Yong-wan that night. Instead of *Romance of the Three Kingdoms*, he finished the detective novel he'd been reading. The clock in the living room struck twelve when he read the last page and closed the book. At that moment, the sound of a small rock, or perhaps a pebble or clump of dirt falling onto a taut piece of paper, came from the direction of the ceiling. It wasn't loud, but the boy jumped because it was late at night. That was the most shocking event that took place on the first of those three days.

The next day, nothing unusual happened except that school was cancelled. His parents forbade him to leave the house. It was quiet outside. It was bi-

"어치케 전기로 밥 비베 묵는다요, 밥 바꿔 묵지?"

"참말로. 비베 묵고 말아 묵고 배 터져서 쌈질이지, 갈라 묵고 바꿔 묵고 함께 살면 왜 싸울까."

"다 일랍디여."

그는 종을 잡을 수 없었다. 왜 싸우냐? 남아서 싸우냐, 모자라서 싸우냐? 누가 싸우냐? 남북이 싸우냐, 군경이 싸우냐, 그 넷이 또 갈라져서 노론소론이 싸우냐? 전쟁이란 항상 멀리서는 보이지만, 가까이서는 안 보이냐? 멀리 떨어지면 누가 왜 싸우는지 전쟁이 보이지만, 가까이 있으면 전쟁은 간 디 없고 먼지와 함성만 있냐? 위오 촉, 삼국시대 사람들은 공명하고 주도독이 싸운 것을 모르고, 어쩌면 유비하고 조조가 싸운 것도 모르고, 그저, 아, 그날도 말들이 먼지를 구름처럼 일으키며 달리는구나, 병졸들이 창을 질질 끌며 걸어가는구나, 잘 익은 대춧빛 얼굴을 한 일기 징수가 적토마를 타고 가는구나, 아, 그러니, 그날도 어디서 또 무슨 싸움이 벌어지고 있구나, 했을 것이다. 그들은 더 알아볼라고 하지 않았을 것이다. 그들은 더 알고 싶지 않았을 것이다. 전쟁은 언제나 있었고, 항상 같았다. 티끌과 고함. 굶주림과 헤어짐. 불안과 공포. 낭비와 황폐. 상처와 죽음. 남

zarre how peaceful it was compared to the day before when the whole day had been riddled with gunshots. There were no mopping operations, no victory processions. No arrests, no recruits. Nothing seemed different on the outside. He observed the adults' reactions. They were also in the dark. Some of them had made it as far as the main street, but all they had to report was news from the alleys.

"I hear they unified northward," the village lady said, returning with her pail of water. She rested it on the wall near the jars and wiped the bottom of the pail with her hand.

"Northward? Dr. Rhee pushed all the way up north?" The boy's mother, who had been scraping the red peel off the yam with a broken spoon, stopped and looked up.

"Charging down, not pushing up." A woman who was sitting on her haunches doing laundry chimed in. "The communists pushed down and won."

"Pushed down? Then it's southward unification."

"How is it southward when the North won? It's northward."

"Sounds like an up-down, topsy-turvy, unforgettable brawl."

"The soldiers pushed down?" The lady washing

나라 말해서 뭣 허냐? 임진년, 병자년, 다 마찬가지. 고려 사람들이 성길사한을 알고, 조선 사람들이 풍신수길을 알았냐? 사실 그때는 고종 같은 이름도, 선조나 인조 같은 이름도 없었다. 왕들이 있었을 뿐. 왕들이란 언제 어디서고 다 같은 사람들. 몽고고 일본이고 후금이고 희랍이고, 또 로마고, 다를 것이 없었다. 임진년에 사람들은 모르면 몰라도 이순신이나 원균을 몰랐다. 혹 이름을 들었더라도, 누군지 몰랐다. 누군지 알았더라도, 얼마나 위대했는지 몰랐다. 적어도 몇 백 년 후 소학교 육학년이 아는 것만큼은 몰랐다. 그가 그때 사람들보다 그 전쟁을 더 잘 아냐? 그는 그때 사람들이 겪었던 전쟁의 고초를 백분의 일도 몰랐다. 그가 그 전쟁을 아냐? 그때 사람들보다 더 잘 아냐? 지금 이 전쟁도, 이것이 필시 전쟁은 전쟁이었다, 어떤 전쟁이고 처음 시작은 가령 구슬 굴리는 소리 같은 것으로 시작되었다, 아마 칠 년 전쟁 첫해 사월 어느 이른 아침, 부산포의 어부들은 까마귀 떼처럼 새카맣게 몰려오는 왜선들을 보고 저것이 갈매기다냐 오륙도다냐 고깃배다냐, 참 별꼴이다, 했을 것이다, 이 전쟁도 십 년이 지나고 백 년이 지나면, 지금 그들이 몰랐던 것들이 속속 볼가져서 선은 이렇고

90

clothes speculated.

"Yes. The soldiers pushed their way down. Who else would invade if not the soldiers?" The lady with the water pail was a little more confident.

"They're the same soldiers..." The laundry lady was skeptical.

"The soldiers were angry and finished off the police," the landlady concluded.

"Aren't they on the same side? Why are they fighting? If they're going to fight, they should keep it to themselves. They shouldn't take innocent lives with them."

"The 38th parallel came down and we were reunitied. If we weren't, how did electricity get all the way down here from the Amnok River? Didn't you have electricity all night last night?" The northward unification lady had evidence to back up her argument.

"The houses that get special treatment aren't so special now, huh? Everyone's getting electricity now. Isn't it special treatment if you get electricity at all hours of the day?" The laundry lady added.

"The electricity we had so far is good enough for me. It's so disorienting to eat by lamplight, you can't tell if the food is going in your mouth or up your

후는 이렇고, 원인은 동인 서인이고 결과는 풍신의 몰락이고, 하면서 금을 그은 듯이 명백하게 모습을 드러낼 것이다. 그때 사람들은 이 전쟁에 대해서 아무것도 모르면서 다 안다고 생각할 것이다. 지금 그가 나중 사람들보다 이 전쟁을 더 잘 알았다, 지금 그는 이 전쟁에 대해서 아는 것이 아무것도 없었지만. 어린 것은 장애가 아니라 장점이었다. 싸움의 쓰라림으로 말하자면, 어린이보다 그것을 더 절실히 겪을 사람이 없었다, 흉년에 새끼 터져 죽고, 에미 보타 죽는다고 하지만. 노인? 늙으면 관심도 감동도 없었다. 살아보면 삶은, 싸움 안 싸움 간에, 그것이 그것이었다. 장년? 그는 바빴다. 그것을, 이기면 이기는 대로, 지면 지는 대로, 이용하느라고 정신이 없었다. 청년? 아, 그는 너무 불쌍했다. 그는 죽느라고 뭘 볼 틈이 없었다. 선배들의 불장난을 항상 젊은이들이 껐다. 장년들이, 심지어 노년들이 침대에서, 책상에서, 광장에서, 강당에서 일으킨 전쟁을, 싫든 좋든, 대개 속아서, 그들이 벌판에서 끝냈다. 소년은? 노장년이 잇속으로, 청년이 몸으로, 치르는 전쟁을 소년은 가슴으로 겪는다. 노장청년이 백 년 뒤 사람들이 잘 알 것을 안다면, 소년은 그들이 도저히 알 수 없는

nose. And the soot from the flame is murder. I'll be happy to get rid of the lamp."

"Food doesn't go up your nose because you eat in the dark. You can eat with your eyes closed!"

"That's true. If I can't eat, it's because there's nothing to eat. Not because it's dark." It was not clear if the laundry lady agreed, or if she just wanted to have the last word.

"Now that we can eat in the light like people instead of eating out of pails in the dark like animals, I realize just how horrible it was that we used to have to eat like that."

"You can eat if it's a little dark, but my boy can't study in the dark. I had to at least find him an oil lamp since we couldn't afford candles."

"Now your boy can study and we can all eat under a light brighter than a hundred candles."

"We used to not get as much light, and if we did, it was about as bright as hanging a persimmon from the ceiling."

"I hear we're short on electricity down here in the South while in the North they have more than enough."

"What do they do with the extra electricity? Eat it with their rice?"

것을 안다. 그는 전쟁을 안다. 그가 아는 것은 세월이 흐를수록 잊혀져서 없어진다. 남는 것은 곰팡이 긴 마른 종이더미들.

"엄니, 군대가 왜 경찰하고 싸운다요?"

"사이가 안 좋은갑다."

"왜 사이가 안 좋다요?"

"싸워쌍께."

"삼팔선 이북에서도 군인들이 경찰서를 쳐들어간다요?"

"아이고, 몰라."

"이북에도 경찰이 있다요? 군대가 있다요?"

"있는갑더라. 이름이 다른갑더라."

"그러면 경찰허고 군대가 없고, 딴것들이 있는갑소."

"그런갑다. 니는 그런 것 몰라도 된다. 돌아다니지 말어라. 성은 방에 있냐? 고구마 삶아줄게, 니도 방에 가 있거라. 총소리 나면 이불을 뒤집어써라. 감 따갖고 얼렁 들어가거라."

"딴것들이 뭣이다요? 순검, 포도, 역졸, 이방이다요? 육진, 도독, 비변, 병조다요?"

"무슨 딴것들? 뭣이 그렇게 많냐? 성한테 물어봐라. 니는 뭔 궁금헌 것이 그렇게 많냐? 당냥 좀 갖고 오니라."

"You can't eat electricity with rice. They sell it for rice."

"For cryin' out loud, they're fighting because they got their bellies full having all the electricity to themselves. If they shared and exchanged some of it, we wouldn't be in this mess."

"If only they'd come to their senses!"

The boy was confused. Why were they fighting? Because they had too much? Too little? Who was fighting? The North and South? The army and the police? Did they split into four and now *noron* and *soron* were fighting, too?[7] Were wars always easier to see from far away, but not up close? From far away, you can see who is fighting and why, but from up close it's all dust and shouting, and no war? During the Three Kingdoms Period, people would not have known that Zhuge Liang and Zhou Yu had gone into battle, or that Liu Biao and Cao Cao had waged any wars. The people must have watched the battles and thought, 'The horses are galloping and great clouds of dust are rising behind them. The foot soldiers are marching and dragging their spears. A commander with a face of the colour of the sun-ripe jujumbe is riding a fast horse. Ah, there must be a battle going on somewhere

"예?"

"당냥 말이다."

"뭣이요?"

"아, 당냥 말이다, 당냥."

"왜요?"

"요, 방정맞은 새끼. 저녁 안 묵을래?"

"고구마는요?"

"아, 당장 당냥 못 갖고 오냐?"

"어디요?"

"어디서 왔냐? 새로 왔냐? 호야랑 다 닦아놨냐, 금방 어두워지는디?"

"성 차렌디."

"묵는 것도 성 차례냐?"

"같이 묵는디."

"일도 같이 허면 안 되냐?"

"호야가 하나뿐인디."

"또 깨묵었냐?"

"성이 깼는디. 오래 됐는디."

"엄니가 뭘 시켰냐?"

"성냥인디."

today.' They would not have tried to find out more. They would not have wanted to know. There had always been wars, and this had not changed. Dust and debris and cries. Starvation and estrangement. Anxiety and terror. Waste and destitution. Injuries and death. One didn't even have to go all the way to China to find war. There were plenty of examples here at home. The war in 1592 and the war in 1636 were much the same. Had the Goryeo people heard of Genghis Khan? Had the people of the Joseon period known who Toyotomi Hideyoshi was? There had been no Kojong, Seonjo, or Injo then; there had simply been kings. Kings were the same regardless of era or location; they were the same in Mongolia, in Japan, in Later Jin, Greece, and Rome. In 1592, people did not know who Yi Sun-sin or Won Kyun was. Even if they did know, they did not know what great men they were. They did not know as well as sixth graders several hundred years later would know. But did the boy know more about the war than they had? He did not know one one hundredths of the actual suffering they had endured. Did he know about war? Did he know the war in 1592 better than those who had lived through it? This war was also undoubtedly a

"그래. 얼렁 갖고 오니라. 훤해서 밥해 묵어뿔자."

"벌써 어두워지는디."

전쟁 둘째 날 밤은 아무 일 없이 저물어갔다. 그날은 전쟁 중에서 가장 전쟁다운 기간이었다. 그는 머릿속이 텅 비도록 아무것도 몰랐다. 사실 그날 오후, 아무 일도 없는 것이 아니었다. 시내 주택가에 박격포탄들이 무차별로 떨어져서 도처에 도리방석만한 구덩이들을 수없이 팠다, 도시 전체를 쏘로 만들지는 못했지만.

사흘째 되는 날 아침이 밝았다. 부엌 옆 지고에서 덕석을 깔고 잠을 잔 그의 식구들 중에서 아마 그가 맨 늦게 일어났다. 그의 어머니는 벌써 가마솥에 밥을 한솥 그득 해놓았다. 그는 얼굴 씻기가 싫었다. 더 자고 싶었고, 일어났다면 쭈그리고 앉아서 멍하니 졸고 싶었다. 그는 밥솥 아궁이 앞에 앉아서 불을 쬐었다. 솔가지를 때서 밥을 지은 아궁이에는 꺼져 가는 잉걸이 벌겋게 재 속에 남아 있었고, 촛불만한 불꽃들이 몇 개 너울거렸다. 그가 땔감을 던져주자 불길이 살아났다. 불길은 곧 사그라졌다. 그는 또 땔감 한 주먹을 던졌다. 또 불길이 솟았다. 그가 시방 아침밥 다 태워뿔래? 예? 밥 탄단 말이다. 밥이요?

war. No matter which war, every war began with, for example, the sound of rolling marbles. Perhaps, on one April morning in the first year of the the Imjin War, fishermen in the Busan harbor saw Japanese ships swarming the horizon like crows, and wondered amongst themselves, 'Are those seagulls, or the Oryuk Islands, or fishing boats? How strange.' In ten or one hundred years, what villagers did not know now would eventually be revealed, the beginning and end recorded, the causes and effects analyzed, and everything will be as clear as day. People in the future will think that they knew everything about this war when they, in fact, know nothing about it. The boy knew this war more intimately than people in the future ever will, even though he did not know anything about it. Being young was not a handicap but an advantage. When it came to the wounds of war, no one was hit harder than children. In times of famine kids are blown up, moms are shrivelled down, to death. The elderly man? He was neither interested nor inspired. Life had taught him that little changed in life, wars or no wars. The man in his prime? He was busy. Whether his side won or lost, he was busy using the situation to his advantage. The

"아이, 야야. 밥 좀 제쳐라. 넘은 지가 너무 됐다."

"예? 밥이요?"

그는 정신이 퍼뜩 들었다. 아마 졸았던 모양이었다. 그는 불을 땠다. 불을 지르는 것은 장난이건 일이건 재미있었다. 등 뒤에서 인기척이 났다. 그는 그의 어머니인 줄 알았다. 부엌문에는 총을 든 군인이 문간을 가득 채우고 서 있었다. 어쩐지 소리가 컸었다.

"나와. 손들고." 군인이 총 끝을 그의 머리통에다 들이댔다. 그는 그가 시키는 대로 했다. 총 앞에서는 동작이 빨라서 편리했다. 그는 그가 총구 끝에서 그렇게 익숙하게 손을 들 수 있으리라고는 생각하지 못했었다. 마치 여러 번 연습을 해본 것 같았다. 딴 식구들과의 통신과 연락은 그때부터 두절되었다. 나중 안 일이지만, 그의 어머니는 입에다 칫솔을 문 채 끌려나왔다. 그는 두 손들을 뒤꼭지에다 대고 한길가로 끌려갔다. 사람들이 집집에서 입은 채, 신은 채, 안 신었으면 벗은 채, 줄줄이 끌려왔다. 열골 물이 모여 냇물을 이루듯이, 골목마다에서 사람들이 꾸역꾸역 끌려나와 길에 때아닌 저자가 섰다. 그들은 두 손들을 든 채 군용 짐차 뒤를 따라갔다. 그들 양쪽으로 그들에게 총을 겨누고 군인들이 드

young man? The poor young man! He died so fast he had no time to see anything. It was always the young man who had to extinguish the fires set by his seniors. The man in his prime, or sometimes even the elderly man, started wars in his bed, at his desk, in the square, and in the auditorium, and the young man was often fooled into going out to the fields and fighting in them, whether they wanted to or not. And the boy? While the elderly man and the man in his prime waged wars for gain, and the young man fought with his body, the boy experienced wars with his heart. While men of all other ages were well aware of the actual facts and details people would remember a hundred years later, the boy experienced what they could never know. The boy knew war. What he knew were forgotten with time and disappeared eventually. What remained were nothing but dry, moldy stacks of paper.

"Mother, why is the army fighting with the police?"

"They don't get along, I guess."

"Why don't they get along?"

"Because they won't quit fighting."

"Do soldiers ambush police stations in the North, too?"

문드문 그들과 함께 걸었다. 돛배 덮개를 한 커다란 짐차에도 총을 겨눈 군인들이 탔다. 그는 인사 한마디 나누지 못하고 부모형제와 떨어져서 포로가 되었다. 그들은 남녀노소 없이 포로들이었다. 그는 우연히 그의 근처에 있는 흥분한 군인의 판단에 따라서 언제든지 삶과 죽음이 갈라질 수 있었다. 군인들은 형편에 따라서 의장대나 군악대처럼 국민들의 노리개나 구경거리가 될 수도 있었고, 지금처럼 국민들을 쫓긴 토끼나 여우로 사냥하는 피를 본 미친 사냥개가 될 수도 있었다. 그들은 둘 다 똑같은 군인들이었고, 더러는 같은 사람들일 수도 있었다. 누가 씩씩하고 정의롭고 예의 바르고 네모반듯한 젊은이들을 피에 주린 아귀로 만들었냐? 그들은 아니었다. 그들한테는 끌려가는 죄밖에 없었다. 군인들은 이틀 전, 비켜, 하고 총질을 해대던 군인들과 똑같은 군대였다. 똑같은 철모, 똑같은 군복, 똑같은 소총, 똑같은 낯짝. 그들은 북쪽으로 이동했다. 그들이 남문다리를 건너서 우편국 앞에 이르렀을 때, 길가에 서 있던 군인들 중 하나가 다가와서 그들 몇을 불러 세웠다. 그는 즉시 시키는 대로 몇 사람들과 함께 줄 밖으로 빠져나갔다. 군인은 그들에게 소방서 건물 위를 가리켰다.

"How should I know?"

"Do they have policemen in the North? Do they have armies?"

"I hear they do. They're called something different, though."

"Then I guess they have something else instead of armies and police."

"I guess so. You don't need to know all that. Don't go running around outside. Is your big brother in his room? I'll steam some yams. You go wait in your room, too. If you hear guns, get under the covers. Hurry up. Get your persimmons and go inside."

"What other things are policemen called? *Sungeom? Podo? Yeokchol? Ibang?* Or *Yukchin? Dodok? Bibyeon? Byeongjo?*"[8]

"What other things? What are all these words? Ask your big brother. Why do you have so many questions? Go get the *dangnyang*."

"Yes?"

"*The dangnyang.*"

"What?"

"*The dangnyang.* Don't you know what *dangnyang* is?"

"Why?"

"저것 보이냐?"

"민족청년단이요?"

"건물 위에 깃발을 떼 온다." 군인은 그를 건너서 그보다 더 큰 아이를 손가락질했다. "너."

나머지는 "원대복귀"해서 다시 북진 포로 대열에 끼여들었다. 소방선가 청년단 건물 위에서 아침햇살을 받으며 나부끼고 있던 깃발은 붉은빛 파란빛 하얀 바탕 붉은 별도 또렷한 인공기였다. 그때까지도 그들은 그들을 잡아가는 군대가 진압군인 줄 몰랐다. 군인들이 철모에 하얀 띠를 둘렀지만 그들은 그것을 눈여겨볼 겨를이 없었다. 왜 깃발을 내리냐? 총알이 씽씽 날아다니는디 무섭겄다. 즈그는 죽기 싫어서 안 올라가고 그들의 북진 행렬은 북소학교에서 끝났다. 거기에는 그들처럼 붙잡혀 온 사람들이 넓은 운동장을 가득 채우고 울타리 밖 벼논 논배미 위에까지 넘쳤다. 그들은 궐기대회 때처럼 한 덩어리로 운동장을 메운 것이 아니라, 무더기 무더기로 나뉘어 집총 군인들의 감시를 받았다. 남자 어른들은 아랫도리 맨속옷 하나만 걸치고 께댕이를 홀딱 벗었다. 무더기와 무더기 사이의 어떤 금은 생사를 가르는 사선인 모양이었다. 벗은 장정들이 손들을 뒤로

"You little...! Don't you want dinner?"

"What about the yams?"

"I said go get *the dangnyang.*"

"Where?"

"Where'd you come from? Are you new to our house? Have you wiped the lamp? It's going to get dark soon."

"It's brother's turn."

"Is it his turn to eat, too?"

"We eat together."

"So can't you both help out?"

"There's only one lamp."

"Did you break it again?"

"Brother did. A long time ago."

"What did your mother just tell you?"

"They're not '*dangnyang*.' They're called 'matches surely.'"

"Fine. Go get them. Let's eat while there's still some light left."

"It's getting dark already."

The second night of the war went by without any new developments. That was the most war-like day of the war. The boy was so unaware of it all that his head felt empty. In reality, something had happened that afternoon. Mortar munitions had hit

묶이고 굴비두름처럼 줄줄이 엮여서 군인들에게 끌려 나갔다. 드르륵 드르륵 총소리들이 간단없이 들려왔다. 그들은 경찰관 옷과 금테모자를 쓴 사람이 군인들과 섞여서 사이좋게 설치는 것을 보고 세상이 또 한 번 뒤집힌 것을 깨닫기 시작했다. 그는 배가 고팠다. 아침나절에는 그럭저럭 구경거리도 많고 해서 배고픈 줄 몰랐는데, 점심때가 겹자 차츰 지루하고 허기가 지기 시작했다. 그는 머리가 텅 비어서 아무것도 알 수 없었다. 처음에는 죽는 사람들은 물론 죽이는 사람들도 들뜨고 격했는데, 나중에는 차츰 죽이는 사람들은 물론 죽는 사람들도 허리가 아프고 놀이가 시들해졌다. 오전 중에는 모든 것이 새롭기도 했지만, 진짜 구경거리가 하나 있었다. 교실들과 운동장 사이에 잎들을 반쯤 쏟고 노랗게 물든 키 큰 나무들이 늘어서 있었는데, 그보다 키가 작아 보이는 학생 하나가 끌려나와 두 눈들을 가리운 채 그중에서 가장 큰 나무의 밑둥 앞에 세워졌다. 그가 어디서 볼가졌는지 아무도 몰랐다. 그가 두 손들을 뒤로 묶인 채 끌려 나올 때만 해도 그를 눈여겨보는 사람은 아무도 없었다. 끌려 나오는 사람들이 어디 한둘인가. 그는 온몸의 피가 거꾸로 흐르는 것 같았다. 맨머리

the downtown residential areas indiscriminately and blew craters the size of sitting mats all over town. Fortunately, they did not leave the entire city in marshes.

The third day dawned. Among the family members who had slept on straw mats in the storage room next to the kitchen, he was probably the last one to rise. His mother had already boiled a pot of rice. He did not want to wash his face. He wanted to sleep a little longer, and if he had to wake up, he wanted to sit and doze for a while. He hunkered down in front of the hearth for the warmth. In the hearth that burned pine branches to make the rice, red embers glowed and a few candle-sized flames danced. He stoked the fire with tinder, and the flames came back to life. Then they relented again. He threw another fistful of tinder in it. The flames rose again. You're burning your breakfast? What? The rice is burning. Rice?

"Add final fire to the rice, child. It's been cooking for too long."

"Rice?"

He suddenly snapped out of it. He must have dozed off. He fed the fire. He always enjoyed handling fire, whether it was work or play. He heard

바람의 군인 하나가 묶인 학생 곁으로 다가갔다. 군인이 머리를 학생의 머리에다가 바싹 댔다. 숨바꼭질 규칙을 정하는 것 같았다. 그가 물러났다. 옆에 있는 딴 군인에게 그가 갑자기 무슨 생각이 떠오른 듯이 뭐라고 중얼거렸다. 딴 군인이 어디론가 사라졌다. 딴 사람들은 드문드문 선 자리에 그대로 서서 마치 누가 나무 등치에 세워진 것을 잊어버리기라도 한 것처럼 멀뚱멀뚱 서로 쳐다보고 말들이 없었다. 금방 나간 군인이 다시 나타났다. 그가 맨머리 바람 군인과 몇 마디 주고받고 묶인 학생께로 다가가서 가지고 온 것을 그의 머리 위로 확 던졌다. 저것이 무엇이냐? 새색시 다홍치마 치마폭이냐, 저승사자 검붉은 도포자락이냐. 곱게 물든 활엽수 교목 저 높은 가지에서 떨어지듯 붉고 푸르고 하얀 바탕 붉은 별이 또렷한 커다란 천 조각이 너울너울 펼쳐져서 학생의 몸을 머리부터 덮었다. 덜 펼쳐지고 구겨진 곳은 손을 못 쓰는 학생을 대신해서 군인이 허리를 굽혀 가며 칠성판에 명정 덮듯 정성스럽게 폈다. 그가 손을 털고 물러났다. 맨머리 바람의 군인 옆에서 지켜보고 있던 군인들 중에서 하나가 앞으로 나섰다. 그가, 누가 오는지 볼 수 없는 학생 앞으로 다가갔다. 그

someone approaching from behind. He thought it was his mother. A soldier carrying a gun filled the threshold. No wonder the footsteps had been so loud.

"Get out. Hands in the air." The soldier aimed his gun at the boy's head. The boy did as he was told. Guns were good for making people move faster. The boy would never have guessed he could raise his hands so instantly with the muzzle of a gun pointed at him. It felt well rehearsed. He lost touch with the rest of his family then. It was not until later that he discovered his mother was dragged out with her toothbrush still in her mouth. He was led to the street with his hands behind his head. People were being dragged out of their houses clothed, half-clothed, with shoes, without shoes. As brooks turn into streams, people poured out of every alley. It felt like a village market. They followed the army truck with their hands behind their heads. Soldiers with guns at the ready were peppered throughout the procession. Soldiers on a large truck with a canvas top also aimed guns at the people. The boy was separated from his family without exchanging farewells, and became a prisoner. Men, women, young and old—they were all

는 서너 걸음 남겨놓고 멈춰 서서 총을 벗어 들었다. 총신만 있고 개머리판이 없는 기관단총이었다. 그가 길쭉한 탄창을 한 손으로 쥐고 총을 어깨에 댔다. 그때까지 수없이 들려왔던 드르륵 드르륵 소리가 그 총 끝에선지 딴 데선지 알 수 없게 돼 번 났다. 바로 그 총구멍 앞에 서 있던 사람이 한옆으로 비스듬히 쓰러졌지만, 그 검은 쇠붙이가 그 무너짐에 책임이 있는 것 같아 보이지 않았다. 그것은 너무 무심했다. 그는 다만 묶인 채 너무 오래 서 있어서, 가령 여름날 뙤약볕에서처럼, 피곤해서 한쪽으로 몸을 눕힌 것뿐이었다. 좀 쉬라고.

해가 학교 옆 산으로 기울자 짧은 가을날이 곧 저물었다. 그는 춥고 배고팠다. 논두렁에 베어 놓은 나락을 훑어서 참새처럼 까먹었지만, 입만 아프고 목구멍으로 넘어가는 것이 없었다. 그가 어리다고 풀려난 것은 날이 어두워진 다음이었다. 그는 논두렁길을 걸었다. 웃논배미 아랫논배미가 그의 키만한 높이로 턱이 졌고, 거기에 벗은 채 총 맞은 피투성이 송장들이 겹겹이 나자빠져 있었다. 그는 무섭지 않았다. 아마 그는 무엇에 너무 가까이 갔었다.

prisoners. He could be separated from the living at any moment according to the discretion of a riled up nearby soldier. The soldiers sometimes entertained people as honor guards and army bands. Other times, they hunted them like bloodthirsty hounds going after rabbits or foxes. They were the same soldiers, and sometimes the very same individuals. Who turned the brave, honorable, polite, and wholesome young men into bloodthirsty demons? Not the villagers. They had done nothing but get dragged out to the streets. The soldiers were from the same army that told the boys to get out of the way just two days earlier. The same helmet, the same uniform, guns, faces. The procession headed north. When they crossed the South Gate Bridge and arrived at the post office, a soldier who was standing on the side of the road stopped them and pulled a few of the villagers out of the rows. The boy stepped out of the row immediately as ordered. The soldier pointed above the fire station building.

"Do you see that?"

"The National Youth Corp?"

"Retrieve the flag from the building." The soldier skipped the boy and pointed at a larger boy, "You."

팔공산

난리가 났다. 그날은 일요일이었다. 경찰서 고동이 대낮에 수십 번 울었다. 처음에는 통금도 해금도 아닌데 웬일인가 했고, 더 계속되자 별일이다 싶었고, 그래도 또 되풀이되자 아무래도 무슨 일이 났는가보다고 덜컥 겁이 났다. 그때는 연습이 없었다. 놀러 온 그의 친구가 자리에서 일어섰다. 그들은 마루 끝에 걸터앉아 환담을 하던 중이었다.

"낼 학교서 만나자."

"어디 알아볼 데 있소?"

그의 친구는 그보다 나이가 댓 살 많았다. 그들은 중학생들이었다. 그는 이학년이었고, 친구는 육학년이었다.

"뭐? 고동소리?"

"그것 아니면 왜 일어났소?"

"나는 지금 이빨이 아파서 치과에 간다."

"공일인디?"

"부러진 이빨이 일요일 알아보냐?"

"이빨은 어쩌다 다쳤소? 싸웠소?"

"생물 선생한테 직사게 맞았다."

The rest "returned to the unit" and rejoined the northward procession of prisoners. The flag that flew in the morning sun over the fire station or the National Youth Corp building was red and blue and white with a vivid red star—a North Korean flag. Until then, they had not known that the army taking them away had been the suppressing army. The soldiers had white bands on their helmets, but the prisoners had not noticed. Why were they taking down the flag? It must have been frightening with all the bullets flying around them. They weren't going up to take it down themselves because they didn't want to die. Their northward procession ended at the North Primary School. People who had been captured filled the vast schoolyard and spilled out of the school gates to a parcel of a neighboring rice paddy. They did not stand as one group as they did at rallies, but were divided into small groups that were guarded by soldiers. The men were stripped down to their underwear. The lines drawn between the clusters of people must have been the lines between life and death. The naked men had their hands tied behind their backs and then were joined together by a rope that linked together them like a string of dried fish.

"대대장을 때린다요, 아무리 선생이라고?"

"야, 교장실에 속옷 바람으로 들어가는 것은 전교에서 나밖에 없다."

"교장실에 목욕탕이 있소?"

"운동허다가 급히 부르면 언제 옷 갈아입냐?"

그는 학교 대표 축구선수 수비였다. 별명은 쇠꽂다리였다. 그의 철통같은 다리에 걸리지 않는 공이 없다는 뜻이었다.

"그런 학생을 젊은 선생이 왜 때렸다요, 늙은 선생도 아니고?"

"그런 학생이니까 때렸겠지. 선배 몰라본다고 치더라. 생물실 앞을 지나가는디, 야, 너 잠깐 들어와, 허길래 멋도 모르고 들어갔더니, 느닷없이 주먹뺨이 여지없이 들어오더라. 허천나게 맞았다."

생물 선생은 그 학교 일회 졸업생이었다.

"가만있었소?"

"피했지. 발길이 들어오더라. 축구선수헌테 말이다."

"실험실 근처는 얼씬을 말아야 되겠소?"

"니도 당했냐?"

"아니요. 나는 찹쌀떡을 줍다."

They were led out of the schoolyard. *Ratatat. Ratatat.* The guns sounded without pause. As they watched the men in their police uniforms and golden brimmed hats mingle with the soldiers, the people knew that the world was being turned upside-down once again. The boy was hungry. In the morning, there was much to see and to distract him, but he was bored and hungry by lunchtime. His head was so empty he could not know anything. At first, the dying and even the killers were excited and impassioned, but later on, the dying as well as the killers had backaches and found the game dull. Everything was new in the morning, and there was one diversion. Between the classrooms and the schoolyard was a row of trees that had already shed half its leaves. A boy in a blindfold, shorter than the boy, was taken to the tallest of the trees and placed in front of the tree trunk. No one knew where he had suddenly appeared from. No one was paying attention to him when he was dragged out with his hands tied behind his back. So many had been dragged out into the yard. The boy felt blood rushing to his head. A soldier with no hat approached the boy. The soldier bent down, his head very close to the blindfolded boy's

"떡?"

"수업 끝나고, 실험도구 들고 따라오라고 해서 따라갔
더니, 주먹을 내밉디다. 챙피해서 얼른 도망쳐 나와뿌
렀소."

"심부름은 주번을 시키지 급장을 시키냐? 미안해서
떡 쪼가리 한 개 집어줬는갑다."

"칠판에 영어를 쓰는디, 더듬더듬 따라 읽어봤더니,
알코홀이 됩디다. 얼른, 알콜요, 하고 대답했더니, 누가
영어 젤 잘허냐? 하고는 공치사를 헙디다."

"영어는 니 아니냐?"

"나보다 잘허는 애가 없었어요?"

"그럼 그 애를 데리고 가서 떡을 주지?"

"그 애는 귀싸대기 터졌어요. 건방지다고."

"니는 상을 탔지 않냐?"

"그건 영어 선생한테요. 영어 선생은 못하면 소두방
뚜껑 같은 손으로 뺨을 때리고, 잘허면 호주머닛돈으로
영어 문법책 사서 상 주요. 그것이 신상필벌이다요."

"공부 못헌다고 치고 건방지다고 박는 건 좋은디, 지
나간다고 패면 성헐 놈 어디 있겄냐? 왜 누군 떡 주고
누군 패냐?"

116

head. They looked like they were deciding on hide-and-go-seek rules. The soldier stepped away. He suddenly turned to a soldier nearby and muttered to him as though he had just remembered something. The nearby soldier went off somewhere. The people in the yard stood in clusters and looked at each other wordlessly as though they had forgotten that there was a boy standing alone under the tree. The soldier returned. He exchanged a few words with the helmet-less soldier and then walked over to the blindfolded boy and threw something over his head. What was it? A new bride's ruby-red skirt, or the Messenger of Death's crimson cape? Like a single leaf falling from the lovely tinted tree, a piece of cloth, red and blue and white and decorated with a single vivid red star, opened over his head and fluttered down. It covered the blindfolded boy from the head down. A soldier straightened out the folded and wrinkled corners on behalf of the blindfolded boy who had his hands tied. The soldier was scrupulous about his task, as though he was lining the bottom of a coffin with a funeral banner. He dusted his hands and stepped away. A soldier next to the helmet-less soldier who had been watching all of this

"지나간다고 팼겄소? 잔뜩 꼬느고 있는 판에 눈앞에 얼른거린 것이 죄요."

"야, 공금도 아니고 사재 털어서 그 많은 학생들 상 사 주다가는 월급 어디 남겄냐?"

"상 주는 건 한 번. 딱 한 번, 한 학생. 돈 안 드는 귀뺨 은 골고루 여러 번 멕이지만."

"니, 동기허고 싸웠냐? 맞았냐?"

"상급생하고 어떻게 싸우요? 동기 형하고는 말다툼만 했소."

"딴 애한테 맞았냐? 누구헌테 터졌냐?"

"맞기는 맞았는디, 누군지는 모르요."

"눈 감고 맞았냐? 여럿이 때리더냐?"

"누가 무슨 시자다요? 아침에 등교해서 막 교실에 들 어가는디, 삼학년 똘마니 하나가, 야, 니, 이리 좀 와, 허 고 즈그 교실로 날 데리고 갑디다. 문을 들어서자마자 빈 책가방을 머리 위에 뒤집어씌우고 여기저기서 주먹 들, 발길들을 날리는디, 생각보다 덜 아픕디다."

"맞을 줄 알았냐?"

"아니요, 주먹이 들어올 때도 이것이 뭣인고 했소."

"니는 나 때문에 선배들한테 터지고, 나는 니 때문에

stepped forward. He approached the blindfolded boy who could not see if anyone was coming toward him. The soldier stopped three or four paces away from the tree where the blindfolded boy stood and took the rifle off his shoulder. It was a submachine gun that had no butt plate. He held up the long magazine with one hand and placed the gun on his shoulder. The *ratatat ratatat* that the boy had heard so many times that day sounded a few times from the barrel of that gun or from somewhere else, the boy did not know where. The blindfolded boy standing right across from the barrel fell to his side, but it did not seem as though that black piece of metal could have been responsible for his fall. It had been too nonchalant. It was more likely he had decided to lie on his side because he was tired after being bound and left to stand there for so long, the way people get tired after standing under the blazing summer sun for a long time. He just needed a bit of rest.

When the sun set over the hills on the side of the school, the short autumn day came to a close. The boy was hungry and cold. He got a handful of raw rice from the harvest that was piled along the paddy ridges. Like a bird, he peeled the husks and ate

선생한테 깨졌다. 동기허고는 왜 싸웠냐? 그놈이 입심이 주먹심보다 쎈 놈인디, 니가 입을 뻥긋이라도 했겠냐? 묶어 놓고 권투했냐?"

"상급생이 하급생 앞에서 잘나지 않으면 어디서 잘나졌소? 나는 장단만 맞춰줬소."

"맞는 것도 억울헌디, 가만있으면 반항한다고 생각한다. 생물 선생도 적당히 피하는 척해줬더니 신이 나는 모양이더라. 권투선수는 맷집 좋은 놈이 이긴다."

"때리는 건 폭력이고, 맞는 것은 예술이요."

"예술이사 되겠냐만, 종교쯤은 안 되겠냐? 당신 뜻대로 되소서. 당신 뜻이 이루어지소서. 당신 뜻이 되소서."

"어디서 배웠소?"

"부흥회에 따라가서 어깨 너머 들은 풍월."

"동기한테 끌려갔소? 동기 형의 포교는 위로 선배에 이르고 아래로 후배에 미쳐요. 가위 무소부지요. 한 손에 성전, 또 한 손에 칼, 말로 안 되면 주먹을 휘두르요. 성전은 말, 칼은 주먹 아니요?"

"주먹을 휘두르더냐, 니한테?"

"입주먹은 주먹 아니요?"

"입은 말이고 주먹은 폭력이지. 말로 안 되면 폭력을

the grains, but his mouth hurt and he could not swallow anything. It was after dark when he was released. He was too young. He walked along the paddies. On the upper paddies, the naked, bloody corpses of the people who had been shot that day lay in piles as tall as the boy's height. The boy was not scared. Perhaps he had gotten too close to something.

Palgongsan

Turmoil came. It was Sunday. The police station siren sounded a dozen times in broad daylight. People first wondered why the sirens were ringing nowhere near curfew or curfew lift, and then thought something was amiss when the sirens kept going. They began to feel frightened when the sirens persisted. This was before drills. The boy's friend who was visiting got up to leave. They were having a pleasant conversation on the porch.

"I'll see you at school tomorrow."

"Where are you off to?"

The boy's friend was about five years older. They were in secondary school. The boy was a second

쓰는디, 말허고 폭력이 어떻게 같냐? 말로 하란 말은 폭력을 쓰지 말란 말 아니냐?"

"말이라고 다 같은 말이요? 대추씨만헌 붓끝이 역시 대추씨만헌 총알보다 더 무서운 줄 모르요? 사람을 다 치고 죽이는 데는 세 치 혓바닥만한 것이 없소."

"붓은 칼보다 강하다는 말은 붓하고 칼이 다르다는 말 아니냐? 말하고 총이 같으면 더 무섭고 덜 무섭고가 없지."

"말이 폭력 노릇을 할 양이면 총보다 더 잘하는 수도 있고, 총도 쓰기에 따라서는 말보다 더 평화로울 수 있다는 말이요."

"말이라고? 독도 잘 먹으면 약이고, 약도 잘못 먹으면 독이다."

"그러니 아예 잘 먹으면 약, 잘못 먹으면 독이라고 해 뽑시다."

"약방에 독극물 진열장은 어쩌고? 해골바가지는 어쩌고?"

"모든 약병에다가 해골바가지허고 정강이뼈 두 개를 그립시다."

"약방에다가는 적십자 대신에 하얀 두개골 그림을 붙

year, and his friend was a sixth year.

"Do I hear sirens?"

"I thought that was why you got up."

"No, I'm going to the dentist's. I have a tooth-ache."

"Today's Sunday."

"Broken teeth don't care what day of the week it is."

"What happened? Did you get in a brawl?"

"The biology teacher beat the lights out of me."

"Hit the battalion commander? Sure, he's a teach-er... but can he do that?"

"I'm the only one in the whole school who goes to the principal's office in his underwear."

"Do you bathe there?"

"He pulled me out of practice saying it's urgent. I didn't have time to change."

He was the goalie of the school soccer team. His teammates called him Iron Legs. No ball ever got past Iron Legs.

"Why would a young teacher hit a student like you? I could understand if the teacher was old..."

"Exactly because I'm 'a student like me.' He said I didn't show enough respect to an old school alum. I was passing by the biology lab when he said,

이고? 오는 손님도 쫓게?"

"원래 십자가는 형틀 아니요? 그것 벽 한복판에 걸어
놔도 사람들 많이만 몰려듭디다."

"그 집 십자가야 세로가 길지. 적십자도 십자가에서
나왔냐? 약방 적십자가 예수 고생한 십자가냐? 치과 적
십자도 그러냐?"

"병원은 약방 큰집 아니요? 백골 정강이뼈 두 개 가로
지른 것 반듯이 세우면, 예수 못 박은 곤장틀 아니라도,
백십자요."

"야, 이빨이 아파서 죽는 수도 있냐?"

"아파서가 뭐요? 빼다가도 죽소."

"그건 생이빨이지. 썩은 이빨이나 흔들리는 이빨은 밥
먹다가도 뱉어낸다."

"병든 이빨이 이빨이요? 부러진 이빨도 이빨이요? 아
무 걱정 말고 눈 찌끔 감고 가서 뽑아뿌시오."

"니 치과의사 다 됐다. 아프요? 아프지만 참으시오."

"그건 윤 간호요."

"아픈디 어떻게 참냐?"

"의사야 안 아프지요."

"윤 간호는 어떻게 아냐?"

'You! Come here a second.' And I fell for it. His swung his fist at me out of nowhere. He smacked the hell out of me."

The biology teacher was in their school's first graduating class.

"So you just stood there?"

"I ducked. Then he kicked me. A soccer player getting kicked—I'll be damned."

"Steer clear of the biology lab from now on, huh?"

"Did he get you, too?"

"Nah, he actually gave me a sticky rice cake."

"Rice cake?"

"After class, he told me to gather the lab equipment and follow him. So I followed him to the office and he gave me a piece of rice cake. I was so embarrassed I ran out of there."

"Maybe he felt sorry he made the class monitor do what the student on duty was supposed to do."

"He wrote something on the board in English, so I made out the word. It turned out to be 'alcohol.' I quickly answered, 'Alcohol,' and he teased me by asking, 'Who's this English genius?'"

"Aren't you the best at English in your class?"

"Of course not. There's another kid."

"오회 졸업생인가, 양놈같이 생긴 사람 있지요? 얼굴이 하얗고, 살이 찌고, 눈이 부리부리하고, 손등에 털이 나고, 머리가 꼬실이고? 원숭이 손 같은 손으로 윤 간호 엉덩이를 철썩 때립디다."

"니 본 데서?"

"환자는 어리고, 의사는 친군디, 꼬실이가 두려울 것이 무엇이요?"

"의사가 왜 오회 친구나?"

"조수는 의사 아니요? 의사는 의사라고 안 하고 원장이라고 허요."

"원장은 없었냐?"

"출타중이었소. 원장은 명사라 항상 바빠요. 경찰 촉탁의로 경찰서에 갔을 것이요."

"북중학교에서 국민학교 대항 축구시합 심판도 보더라."

"어린 환자는 간호원 제복 밑으로 드러난 종아리를 훔쳐보는 것만으로도 미안해서 주눅이 들었소. 보이는 것을 안 볼 수도 없고. 그는 겁김에 조금 전에 간호원 누나가 주사 놓으면서 그에게 한 말을 고스란히 돌려줬소. 아프요? 아프지만 참으시오. 여자는 속이 있어서 가

126

"Then why not pull *him* aside for a rice cake?"

"He slapped that kid. Said he was cocky."

"Didn't you receive a prize?"

"That was from the English teacher. The English teacher slaps you with his pot-sized hands if you're bad at English, but dips into his own pocket to buy you an English grammar book if you're good. Punishing the bad, rewarding the good."

"I'm fine with punching a dumb student and slapping a cocky one, but what about a kid who's just walking by? How come one gets punched and the other gets a rice cake?"

"He didn't punch you because you were walking by. Your only crime was that you happened to be walking by when he was in a bad mood."

"Your English teacher, by the way, won't have any money to live on if he keeps dipping into his pocket to buy students grammar books."

"He did that once. Only once, to one student. The slaps he doles out generously. Those don't cost him anything."

"Did you fight with Dong-gi? Did he hit you?"

"I wouldn't dare fight an upperclassman. We just argued."

"Did someone else hit you? Who knocked you

만있고, 남자가 어른 위세 대고 째려보는디, 좀 뻔뻔해
보입디다."

"누군가? 육상선수 백?"

"아니요. 운동선수가 뚜부살 찌겄소?"

"맞다. 은행원 조."

"은행서기요? 그 잘난 풍채에? 의사나 외교관을 헐 걸
그랬소. 이빨은 많이 아프요?"

"참고 있다."

"아픈 것을 참으면 쓰요?"

"아픈 것이 아니라 병원에 가는 것 말이다. 안 가고 나
을 수 없냐? 된장을 찍어 바르면 안 되냐? 옛날 치과 없
을 때는 어떻게 살았냐?"

"참말이요. 개썹 오르면 해 뜰 때 탱자나무 울타리 까
시쟁이한테 부탁하면 낫는디, 지금은 무조건 병원에 가
서 양쪽 엉덩이에 주삿바늘을 쿡쿡 찔러대니 사람 상허
겄소."

"니는 애가 어찌 아파도 추접시럽게 아프냐?"

"왜요? 눈꼽 조깨 낀 것이 어째서요? 발등 찧을깨미
겁나요?"

"이가 한본 애려봐라. 귀가 애리든지. 귀 애린 것은 반

around?"

"I did get beat up, but I don't know who it was."

"Did you get beat up with your eyes closed? Were there a lot of them?"

"What is this? An interrogation? I was on my way to the classroom in the morning when a third year called me and took me to his classroom. As soon as the door opened, someone threw a book bag over my head and then fists and feet came at me from all directions. It actually didn't hurt that much."

"Did you know they were going to beat you up?"

"No. Even after the first blow, I didn't know what was going on."

"You got beat up by the older boys because of me, and I got beat up by the teacher because of you. Why'd you argue with Dong-gi? His words are stronger than his punches. You probably couldn't get a word in edgewise. Did he knock you out?"

"Upperclassmen never get to look intimidating except when they're standing next to a group of underclassmen. I played along."

"It's bad enough getting beat up, but they always take it as a sign of defiance if you don't flinch. I ducked a little for the biology teacher, and boy, was he excited. When it comes to boxing, victory

미치꽹이, 이 애린 것은 온미치꽹이단다. 눈꼽 낀 것도
병이냐? 그것도 아프다고 병원에 가냐?"

"귀좆 내린 데는 친구도 없다요. 많이 아픈 것도 자랑
이요?"

"내가 왜 이러고 있냐? 여기서 이러고 있으면 치과에
안 가도 되면 얼마나 좋겠냐?"

"여기 있으면 병원에 안 가도 돼요. 여기 있으면서 어
떻게 치과에 간다요? 여기 있기 아니면 병원에 가기요."

"야, 너 천지개벽이란 말 들어봤냐?"

"또 종교요? 태초에 말쌈이 있었으니……."

"아니, 그 반대."

"종말?"

"그래, 말세."

"아이고, 병원 조깨 가기 싫다고!"

"너도 한본 아파봐라. 세상이 다 싫다. 왜 이빨 한 개
가 부러졌는디 온몸이 흔들리고 열이 나냐?"

"이빨이 화가 났소. 방아 실컷 찧어봤자 노는 배만 살
이 찌니, 일헌 공은 간 디 없고 뼉따구만 남았구나. 이빨
인들 골낸다고 나무랠 수 있으리요."

"이가 노하는 것은 알겠다. 평소 고생에 푸대접이 아

goes to whoever can take a punch."

"Hitting is violence, but being hit is art."

"I don't know about art, but it can be a religion. Thy will be done. Done will thy will be. Be thine will."

"Where'd you learn that?"

"Followed a friend to a church revival and picked up a thing or two there."

"Did Dong-gi drag you to it? Dong-gi's evangelism extends to his seniors and juniors alike. Truly knows no bounds. Bible in one hand, sword in the other, so to speak. Hits you if words don't work. The bible is the word, and the sword is the fist, no?"

"Did he sock you one?"

"Verbal punches hurt just as much."

"The mouth is the word and the fist is violence. He uses violence if words don't work, so how can words and violence be the same? When someone says, 'Let's talk about this like adults,' it means 'Let's not resort to violence.'"

"Not all words are the same. The tip of a brush the size of a date seed is as deadly as a bullet of the same size. Nothing hurts and kills a person like the tongue."

니더라도, 몸이 동강이 났는디, 니라고 가만 있겠냐? 왜
팔다리며 귀며 목뼈가 쑤시고 결리냐?"

"그것들이 없는 의리 지킨다고 동맹 파업했는갑소."

"나 갈란다. 혼자 많이 영감 같은 소리 해라."

"가실라요? 병원질만 아니라면 붙잡아도 허겠소만,
입 안 사정 급해노니 이야기는 뒷전이요."

그들은 그 뒤로 몇 번 만났겠지만 그의 기억에 별로
없었다. 그가 병원에 갔는지 어쨌는지 분명치 않지만,
그는 틀림없이 이빨이 나았을 것이다. 그들은 얼마 안
되는 나이 차이로, 전쟁을 통해 상당히 다른 길들을 걸
었다. 하급생은 중삼을 거쳐 고등학생이 되었고, 상급
생은 한국군 장교가 되어 전방에 있었다. 또 하나, 위보
다는 두 살 어리고 아래보다는 두 살 많아서 그들 사이
에 끼인 동기는 퇴각하는 인민군에게 징용되어 조선의
의용군이 되었다. 그날 일요일에 시작되어 한 달쯤 뒤
에 그들의 고장을 덮친 삼년전쟁이 소강 교착상태에 빠
졌을 때, 뿔뿔이 흩어졌던 학생들은 헤어진 지 두어 달
만에 다시 모였다. 그들 중에는 더러 손에 총을 가진 사
람들도 있었다. 아무리 난리통이지만, 그리고 몇 천 명
학생들 중에서 몇 명에 지나지 않지만, 학생들이 총

"Doesn't 'The pen is mightier than the sword' imply that the pen and sword are different? If words and bullets are the same, there's no reason to be more afraid or less afraid of one or the other."

"All I'm saying is that words put to violent use can do the job better than any gun, and a gun used to bring peace can do so better than any word."

"Is that so? Poison well-used is medicine. Medicine ill-used is poison."

"So why not call all things well-used 'medicine' and all things ill-used 'poison?'"

"What about the shelf of toxic substances at the pharmacist's? What about the skull sign?"

"Then we put a skull and two shin bones on every medicine bottle."

"And skulls will replace crosses as the pharmacy symbol? Scare away the customers?"

"Wasn't the Christian cross originally a crucifixion stand? Hanging that on the wall doesn't seem to perturb anyone."

"That cross is longer lengthwise. Does the red cross also come from that cross? Is the pharmacist's cross the same one that Jesus died on? How about the cross at the dentist's?"

"The hospital is the main house and the pharma-

기류를 가지고 등교하는 것은 예삿일이 아니었다. 맨손의 대부분의 학생들은 무장한 학생들을 겁먹은 부러운 눈초리로 바라보았다. 하급생들 사이에서 그들은 헛소문들을 타고 영웅들이 되었다. 그들과 보통 학생들 사이에는 넘을 수 없는 금이 있었다. 총 가진 학생들끼리도 차별은 있었다. 장대처럼 길다란 장총을 어깨에 메고 나타난 학생은 학년이 높았는데도, 별로 존경을 받지 못했다. 그가 번 선망은 그가 일으킨 웃음 속에 거의 묻혀버렸다. 저것이 무엇이냐? 차라리 바지게 작대기나 타다 만 부지깽이 짊어지고 나오니라. 아무리 총이 좋다기로 지리산 포수 화승총도 총이냐? 아니, 총이 좋다니, 누가? 누가 그래? 그들은 그들이 총을 좋아하는지 싫어하는지 몰랐다. 그들은 그런 것을 생각해 본 적이 없었다. 그들은 총을 수없이 보았지만 가진 적이 없었고, 신기한 총이 그들의 어린 호기심을 건드렸지만 무지막지한 그것의 파괴력이 그들을 겁먹게 했다. 장총을 멘 학생은 그것을 메기 전에도 조금 푼수였다. 그는 웃을 때 화내고 화낼 때 웃었다. 그들은 그가 장총을 메서 총이 막대긴지, 막대기 같은 장총을 메서 그가 우스갠지, 분간이 안 섰지만, 그 둘이 잘 어울린다고 생각했

cies are its cousins, so they're related. Make a cross with the two shin bones, and you have yourself a white cross. Although, it's not quite like the flogging frame Jesus was nailed to."

"Hey, can you die of a toothache?"

"Not if it's just a toothache. You can die pulling teeth."

"That only applies to perfectly healthy teeth. Rotten or loose teeth can pop out in the middle of a meal."

"A rotten tooth is not a tooth. Neither is a broken one. Don't worry about a thing and go. Get it done and over with."

"You sound just like a dentist. Does it hurt? Hang in there."

"Nurse Yun says that."

"How can I 'hang in there' when I'm in pain?"

"Easy for the dentist to say, huh? He's not the one in pain."

"How do you know Nurse Yun?"

"Do you know that guy who was in the fifth graduating class? The foreign-looking one? White face, pudgy, big eyes, hairy hands, curly hair? He gave Nurse Yun a big ol' slap on the butt with his monkey hand."

다. 똑똑한 학생이 그런 총을 멨으면, 총이 돋보일까, 학생이 바보가 될까? 이 멍청한 물음의 대답은 간단했다. 그런 학생은 그런 총 안 멨다. 장총 멘 학생은 의용경찰대에서 왔다.

다음은 스위스 출신 기독교 개혁자의 것과 비슷한 이름을 가진 아담한 소총을, 그것도 그와 같은 학년인 어린 중학생이 들고 나타났다. 그 총은 두 가지 종류들이 있었는데, 그 총 하나는 한국경찰의 기본화기로 반자동식이었고, 그 총 둘은 하나보다 훨씬 귀한 온자동식이었다. 자동은 반자동보다 탄창이 길었다. 반자동은 탄창이 한 주먹 속에 들어갔지만, 자동은 그 주먹 밑으로 비죽이 굽어서 앞으로 주먹 속에 있는 것만큼이나 더 삐져나왔다. 반자동은 단발이지만, 자동은 연발이었다. 정확히 말하자면, 반자동은 단발밖에 안 되었지만, 자동은 반자동, 자동 마음대로 되었다. 연발이면 기관총 아니냐? 그것은 기관단총이었다. 소년이 들고 나온 총이 바로 이 그 총 둘이었다. 그들의 시선들은 선망을 넘어 찬탄으로 빛났다. 그 소년은 부산 미군부대에서 가동, 말하자면 마당쇠 노릇을 하다가 왔다.

그 다음은 권총이었다. 권총은 딴 총들과 격이 달랐

"When you were looking?"

"The patient was young and the doctor was his friend. Nothing could stop Curly."

"How is the doctor friends with someone from that class? Isn't he a bit too young?"

"The assistant is also a doctor. The head doctor goes by 'director.'"

"Where was the director?"

"He was out. He's famous and always busy. He was at the police station as their part-time physician."

"He also refereed the primary school soccer games at North Secondary."

"I, the young patient, was embarrassed and ashamed that I snuck a peek at the nurses bare legs below the nurse's uniform. I could not stop myself from seeing what was there before my eyes. He said to her exactly what she had said to him earlier as she gave him his injection. 'Does it hurt? Hang in there.' The woman kept a dignified silence, and the man glared at me. Shamelessly tried to intimidate me with his seniority."

"Who was it? Paek the track star?"

"No. Athletes don't have jiggly bits like he does."

"I know. Cho the bankteller?"

다. 그들에게 알려진 유일한 권총인 구경 점 사오 권총이 학교에 나타났다. 아마 형이나 삼촌 것을 잠깐 빌려 차고 나온 모양이었다. 그것은 총알이 소총알에 비해서 절반 정도로 짧은 대신에 직경이 거의 배나 되었다. 소총알은 도토리만하고 그 권총알은 엄지손가락 끝만 했다. 만일 탄알이 그 권총알만큼 굵고 소총알만큼 길다면 무엇이 될까? 그런 괴물을 쏘는 총은 총이 아니라 기관포였다. 그것은 개인화기가 아니라 공용화기였다. 땅 위에서 쏘면 나는 비행기를 떨어뜨렸고, 비행기 날갯죽지 밑에다 달면 달리는 자동차를 뒤집어엎었다. 물론 그 권총은 위력 때문이 아니라 위엄 때문에 명성이 높았다. 전쟁 전 그들은 중학교에 입학하자 군사훈련을 받았다. 그들에게 교련을 시킨 악명 높은 유지(얼굴에 구멍이 많아서)는 쇠꽂도 아니고 나무도 아닌 짧은 지휘봉으로 소년들 등짝을 후려치는 것으로 만족했는데, 그곳의 딴 학교의 한 배속장교는 허리 뒤춤에 소불알처럼 축 처진 권총을 차고 다녔다. 똑같은 배속장콘데 누구는 권총이고 누구는 막대기냐. 그들은 총 가진 사람이 막대기 가진 사람보다 학생들 통솔하기가 훨씬 수월할 것이라고 생각했다. 그 학교 학생들한테 그것을 한번

"A bank clerk? With his status and size? A doctor or diplomat would suit him better. How's that toothache?"

"Hanging in there."

"You shouldn't ignore pain."

"I'm not ignoring the pain. I'm trying to avoid the dentist. Is there no way to get better without seeing the dentist? How about dabbing bean paste on it? What did people do in the old days when there were no dentists?"

"It used to be if you got a sty, you could wish it away at dawn with a branch from a thorn bush at a hardy orange fence. Now, people go to the hospital for everything and get injections in both cheeks. Can't be good for the body."

"Your ailment is disgusting."

"What's so disgusting about a little eye booger? Better than stubbing your toe."

"There's nothing worse than an earache or a toothache. You have an earache, it drives you half mad. You have a toothache, it drives you all the way mad. An eye booger is not an ailment. No one goes to the hospital for that."

"Evil spirits blind people to everything else. You want a medal for being in pain?"

물어보려고 했는데 그들은 그렇게 하지 못했다. 그것은 아마 그렇게 중요한 일이 아니었다. 어느 날 그들은 그 장교의 권총에 탄창이 없는 것을 보았다. 시내 학생들이 다 모이는 무슨 궐기대회였는데, 우연히 그들 곁을 지나는 그의 허리에 매달린 검게 손때가 묻은 가죽집을 보았을 때 권총 손잡이의 밑구멍이 텅 비어 있었다. 그들은 그 학교의 학생들한테 그 장교에 관해서 물어볼 필요가 없었다. 탄알집 없는 빈총은 알맹이가 없는 껍질이었다. 빈 껍질은 없는 것만 못했다. 그것은 없는 것을 더 돋보이게 만들었다. 없으면 잊기나 했다.

옛날, 전쟁 전, 그의 학교와 농고가 농고 운동장에서 축구시합 결승전에 붙었을 때, 그들이 한참 노래를 부르며 목이 터져라 응원을 하고 있는데, 경기장 밖 운동장 한쪽 모퉁이에서 탕, 총소리가 나고 사람들이 우, 몰려갔다. 농고 학생인가 졸업생이 한 학교가 패색이 짙은 것에 격분해서 하늘에다 대고 권총을 쏘았다. 시합은 난장판이 되고 그들은 다 이긴 경기를 놓쳤다. 그때는 그런 때였다. 그 무렵, 또 한번은, 남소학교에서 친선경기차 축구시합이 벌어졌는데, 광주에 있는 통신학교하고 하동에 주둔한 보병부대하고 쌈박질이 붙었다. 아

"What am I doing here? I wish if I dawdled for longer I wouldn't have to go to the dentist's."

"If you're here, you can't go to the dentist's. You can't be here and at the dentist's at the same time. It's either here or the hospital."

"Have you ever heard of the Creation of the Heavens and the Earth?"

"Religion again? 'In the beginning, there was the Word...'"

"No, the opposite."

"The end of the world?"

"Yes, the apocalypse."

"All this over a trip to the dentist's!"

"You don't know what I'm going through. I hate the world because of this toothache. It's just one broken tooth, and yet it makes my entire body boil and shake."

"The tooth is angry. Doing all that grinding work day after day. And for what? The guts get fat doing nothing while the tooth works itself to the bone. You can't blame the tooth for being sullen."

"I understand the tooth's anger. It toils for little recognition day after day. And then, on top of all that, it gets broken in half. I'd be angry, too. But why do my arms, legs, ears, and neck hurt because

마 결승전도 아니었다. 통신학교 교장은 별 하나짜리였고, 보병 연대장은 말뚝 셋이었다. 교육부대의 별은 허리의 권총을 뽑아 휘두르다가, 공비토벌 사람사냥으로 눈이 뒤집힌 벌건 손의 전투부대 대령과 그 일당의 등등한 살기 앞에 기가 죽어, 돛배 덮개를 떼어내고 합판으로 검정 뚜껑을 얹은 사분의 일 톤 전용차를 몰고 벌건 별판을 연 채 광주로 퇴각했다. 그때는 참으로 그런 때였다. 그들은 그들의 학교에 나타난 권총이 누구의 것인지는 물론, 그것을 가지고 온 학생이 누구인지도 몰랐다. 그런 것은 아무래도 좋았다. 중요한 것은 권총이 학교에서 학생의 손에 있었다는 것이었다. 누구면 대수냐. 그것이 그가 아닌 한 누구가 누가 되었든 어차피 마찬가지였다.

전쟁이 나자 학교는 문을 닫았다. 그들의 학교도 참 팔자가 기구망측했다. 그는 이차 세계전쟁이 막바지에 이르렀을 때 학교(그때는 소학교)를 만주서 패퇴하는 일본군 막사로 내주고 학교 옆 천주교 선교당에서 공부를 했다. 남의 집처럼 그의 학교를 기웃거리면 긴 칼 찬 군인들과 번들번들한 살찐 말들이 운동장을 메웠다. 중학교 때는 한국군한테 교사를 빼앗기고 그들은 동국민학

of it?"

"Solidarity. They're going on strike to show what little support they have for each other."

"I'm going. I'll leave you to your nonsense."

"So soon? Ahem. If it weren't for thine ailment, I would be so very vehement. But your tooth presently beckons. My tale, alas, comes second."

They must have seen each other a few times after that, but the boy could not remember. The boy didn't know if his friend eventually went to the dentist's or not, but his tooth would certainly have healed anyway. Their slight difference in age led them down very divergent paths in the war. The underclassman went on to high school, and the upperclassman was stationed in the front as an officer in the South Korean army. Dong-gi, who was two years younger than the older one, and two years older than the younger one, was recruited by the retreating North Korean army to be a volunteer soldier.

When the three-year Korean War that began on that very Sunday and found their village a month later came to an impasse, the students who had dispersed to hide re-emerged and congregated for the first time in two months or so. Some of them

교 앞 길가의 커다란 창고에다가 책·걸상들을 들여놓고 공부를 했다. 역사 선생한테 뺨을 맞은 한 상급생이 맞을 짓을 한 것은 생각 않고 맞은 것만 분히 여겨 그들의 역사시간에 창고의 양철 지붕에다가 주먹만 한 돌을 던졌다. 돌은 장마 때 돌담 무너지는 소리를 내면서 지붕을 굴러 내려갔다. 그들은 처음에는 놀랐지만 곧 사태를 알아차리고 선생의 눈치를 살피면서 킥킥 웃었다. 따분한 수업이 중단되고 지연된 것만으로도 즐거운 일이었는데, 빈틈을 보이지 않는 완벽한 무서운 늙은 선생이 생각 밖의 돌발 사태에 낭패를 보인 것은 그들이 감히 기대하지 않았던 과외의 기쁨을 그들에게 주었다. 학교를 뺏기지 않았을 때는 더러 밤에 학교로 몰려가서 그들의 배움터를 그들의 힘으로 밤새워 지켰다. 그것은 학교서 시켜서 한 일이었지만, 재미있었다. 낮에만 다니는 학교에 밤에 전깃불을 켜고 있는 것은 안 하던 짓이라 신이 났고, 어둠 속에 도사린 공포 섞인 신비가 어린 모험심을 건드렸다. 어린 그는 학교 밖에서도 야경을 했다. 집에 장정이 없으면 돈을 내거나 아녀자라도 나가서 한몫을 해야 했다. 차례가 아닌데 나가면 돈을 주었다. 그는 그 재미로 더러 팔려서 번을 섰다. 일이라

carried guns. Even though the country was at war and there were only a few guns among over a thousand students, it was no small matter that students were bringing guns to school. The unarmed students regarded the armed ones with fear and envy. False rumors circulated among the underclassmen, and the gun-carrying students were regarded as heroes. An impenetrable line was drawn between these students and the rest of the school. A hierarchy was established even among the ones who carried guns. The boy who turned up with a long rifle the length of a pole slung over his shoulder was not very respected in spite of his age. What little envy he had earned was drowned in jeers from the other gun-toting students. What is that? Might as well carry around an A-frame carrier cane or a half-burnt wooden poker. Sure, guns are nice, but a boonie hunter's firelock rifle is not a gun! Guns are nice? Says who? Who says guns are nice?

They didn't know whether they liked guns or not. The question had never occurred to them. Guns were always around, but they had never owned any. Guns piqued their juvenile curiosity, but their enormous destructive power scared them. The boy

야 아래쪽에서 지르는 소리를 위쪽으로 옮기고, 위쪽에서 오는 소리를 아래쪽으로 보내면 되었다. 그 소리는 대개 이상 없다고 전달, 이었다. 어려울 것이 없었다. 뒤번 밤잠을 설치고 나면 참고서가 한 권 생겼다. 그는 영어 문법책을 샀다. 국어사전은 없어도 영어사전은 있었고, 국문법책 살 생각은 못 했어도 영문법책은 진즉부터 벼르던 책이었다. 우연히 책뚜껑에 붉은 띠가 둘려 있었다. 그는 그 책을 사서 옆구리에 끼고 집으로 가다가 길에서 낯선 어른의 인사를 받았다. 야, 무슨 책이냐? 예? 영어책이요. 그거 좀 볼꺼냐? 왜 그래요? 조선 걸도 못허는디 왜걸 허냐? 어디 좀 보자. 어른은 말과는 다르게 벌써 그의 책을 거칠게 힘으로 그에게서 나꿔챘다. 그는 책을 펼쳐서 두어 군데 훑어보더니, 보자고 할 때와는 다르게 무뚝뚝하고 불친절하게 책을 그에게 돌려주었다. 어린 그는 무식한 그 남자가 책에 흥미를 가진 것이 기특해서 어렵사리 손에 넣은 그 책을 대낮에 한길에서 뺏기지 않은 것을 다행으로 여길 겨를이 없었다.

전쟁이 임박했다는 말은 그들에게 새삼스러워서 아무 감흥을 주지 못했다. 그들은 그동안 내내 전쟁 속에서 살았다. 난리라는 말이 더 어울렸다. 피난민들이 남

with the long rifle was a bit of a buffoon even before he got himself a rifle. He was angry in funny
moments and laughed during infuriating ones.
Whether the rifle made him ridiculous or the other
way around was not clear, but the students thought
the long rifle suited him. If the long rifle belonged
to a clever student, would it have made the rifle
look better, or the student sillier? There was a
simple answer to this absurd question: clever students never carried those kinds of guns in the first
place. The boy with the long rifle came from the
volunteer police force.

Next, a young middle school boy brought a
compact rifle with a name that sounded like the
famed Swiss religious reformist. There were two
kinds of compact rifles available: one was the
semi-automatic, standard issue in the Korean police force, and the other was the much rarer automatic rifle. The automatic had a longer magazine
than the semi-automatic magazine. The latter fit
right in the palm of one's hand, but the former was
twice as long. The semi-automatic was single shot,
but the automatic could fire multiple shots with one
pull of the trigger. Semi-automatics could only fire
one shot at a time, but the automatic could fire

부여대 꾸역꾸역 몰려드는 것이 난리였다. 사람들은 팔금산으로 가야 목숨을 부지한다는 소문을 들었든 못 들었든, 믿든 안 믿든, 임시수도를 향해서 계속 동쪽으로 발걸음을 옮겼다. 그들도 덩달아 피난 보따리를 쌌다. 보따리는 쌌지만 떠나는 사람은 형편이 좋은 소수였다. 그의 아버지는 그의 어머니의 반대를 무릅쓰고 심사숙고 끝에 아들 둘만 팔금산으로 피난을 보내기로 작정했다. 형편이 다 살 수 없으면 일부라도 살아야 한다는 계산이었다. 그 일부도 사실은 떠날 형편이 못 되었다. 그와 그의 형은 어려서 철이 없었든지, 부명에 감히 거역은 물론 토도 달 수 없었든지, 부모형제를 사지에 남겨두고 어떻게 그들만 살자고 떠나냐고 한바탕 법석은커녕 눈물 바람 콧물 바람 생이별 장면 하나 없이 시키는 대로 고분고분 원족이라도 가는 것처럼 길을 떠났다. 그들은 배낭을 짊어졌다. 그 속에는 음식과 옷가지와 돈 뭉치가 한 다발씩 들어 있었다. 모험치고는 너무 평화스러웠고, 여행치고는 너무 살벌했다. 그는 덤덤했다. 무서운 생각도 안 들었고, 즐거운 마음도 없었다. 무섭기에는 소년의 야망, 소년의 호기심이 현실을 몰랐고, 즐겁기에는 떠나는 곳이나 가는 곳 모두 앞날이 너

single or multiple shots. Then, wasn't an automatic really a machine gun? It was a submachine gun. The young middle school boy had brought a submachine gun to class. The other boys were beyond jealous. Their faces lit up with admiration when he walked in. The boy had served as the house boy— the errand boy—at the U.S. army base in Busan.

Then there were the pistols. A pistol was in a class of its own. The only pistol the boys had heard of, the .45, appeared at school. Someone must have borrowed his older brother or uncle's gun. The bullet was half the length of a rifle bullet, but twice the diameter. A rifle bullet was as thick as an acorn while the pistol bullet was the size of a thumb. What if there was a bullet that wide and long? Guns that could fire such monsters were machine guns. They weren't personal firearms but crew-served weapons. When fired from the ground, they could shoot down planes. Attached under the wings of planes, they could flip cars on the land below.

The pistol, of course, was famous for its reputation, not for its power. Before the war, the boys had received military training when they entered middle school. Their drill instructor was infamous.

무 캄캄했다. 집에 있는 것도 떠나는 것 못지않게 모험
이었다. 어쩌면 더 목숨을 건 모험이었다. 집에 머무는
것이 편하고 지겨운 반복일 때 길 떠나는 것이 전율찬
모험일 수 있었다. 일상에서 빠져나가는 것이 모험이었
다. 지금은 집이 비상이었다. 집을 떠나는 것은 모험을
피하는 것이었다. 한 모험을 떠나서 딴 모험 속으로 들
어가는 것이었다. 큰 모험을 버리고 작은 모험을 찾는
것이었다. 생사를 헤매는 전쟁 속의 모험을 피해서 낯
선 거리를 떠도는 집 없는 천사의 모험을 택하는 것이
었다. 부모형제를 버리고 떠난다는 죄책감이 아니더라
도, 순전히 모험을 좋아하는 소년의 무모한 패기만으로
도 떠나는 것은 비겁했다. 그들의 발걸음은 무거웠다.

남쪽으로 가는 길과 동쪽으로 가는 길이 갈라지고, 그
동쪽 길이 기찻길과 엇갈리는 길목에서 그는 그의 영어
선생을 만났다.

"죽지 않으면 또 만나자." 선생은 커다란 손으로 그의
손을 덥석 잡고 말했다. 그는 제자의 인사를 받고 표연
히 사람들 속으로 사라졌다. 그도 그들처럼 배낭을 짊
어지고 있었다. 그는 그 선생한테 뺨을 맞은 학생들이
그 선생의 손이 크고 손때가 맵다고 투덜대던 것이 생

They called him citron (because of the pockmarks on his face) and he was perfectly happy to literally whip the boys into shape using a short baton that was made of neither metal nor wood. But one military officer assigned to another school in the village carried a gun with him in a holster that hung near his back like bull testicles. How come one drill instructor had a baton and the other a gun? The boys thought that the one with the gun would have an easier time controlling students. They planned to verify this with students from that school but they never got around to it. It was probably not such a pressing question.

One day, the boys noticed that the officer's pistol did not have a magazine. It was at some rally that had all the students from the village gathered. They happened to see as the officer walked by that the pistol in his leather holster, shiny black from years of wear, had a gaping hole where the magazine should be. They no longer needed to ask the students of that school about the officer's influence. A pistol without a magazine was a husk without kernel. A husk was worse than having no gun at all. It drew attention to his shortcoming. No one would have noticed this shortcoming if he'd had no gun at

각났다. 그 선생은 한번은 맨발에 고무신을 신고 교실
에 들어왔다. 학생들은 선생의 발가락 사이에 때가 껴
있는 것을 보았다. 고무신을 신으면 발한이 잘 안 되어
아무리 깨끗한 발이라도 검은 때가 금방 꼈다. 그 선생
은 선생 같기보다는 촌 머슴이나 땔나무꾼 같아 보였
다. 그는 그 선생이 정직하고 성실하고 원칙을 고집하
는 당찬 전문가라는 것을 알았다. 그가 딴 학생들과 함
께 그 선생 흉을 보고 재미있어했던 것은 그 선생한테
배우는 것이 무한히 보장되었기 때문이었다. 그 선생이
기약 없이 부연 먼지 속으로 모습을 감추자 그는 그 선
생이 그들에게 얼마나 중요했는가를 깨달았다. 이상하
게도 죽고 사는 것보다 그 선생에게 다시는 공부를 배
울 수 없을지도 모른다는 생각이 더 그의 마음을 사로
잡았다. 나중 나중 이야기지만, 그는 그 선생에게 배울
기회를 다시는 갖지 못했다. 그가 고향에서 면장을 한
다는 소문을 들었을 뿐이었다.

　그들은 철길을 건너서 사람들을 따라 걸었다. 차들이
지나갈 때마다 손을 들었지만, 멈추는 차는 없었다. 그
들은 생목까지 갔다. 그곳은 그들의 할머니에 의하면
옛날 고름장 모퉁이였다. 늙은 부모를 지게에 지고 와

all.

Long ago, long before the war, the village school and the neighboring agricultural school had a finals soccer match at the agricultural school athletic field. The boys of both schools had been singing and cheering themselves hoarse when they heard a gunshot outside the playing field. People swarmed towards the source of the sound to find that a current student or alumni of the agricultural school had fired a shot into the air, livid that his side was about to lose. The game turned to pandemonium, and the match was forfeited moments before the boy's school was about to achieve victory. It was that kind of time. Around the time of that same incident a communications school in Gwangju and an infantry troop in Hadong got into a fight at another friendly soccer match at the South Primary School. The game wasn't even the finals. The communications school principal had one star (brigadier general) and the regimental commander of the troop had three stripes (captain). The star of the education corps pulled out his pistol and brandished it at them, but then was soon intimidated by the murderous vibe coming from the combat unit and their captain. The captain and his unit had touches of

서 버리고 가는 데였다.

　낮에는 호랭이가 나오고, 부슬부슬 비 오는 밤이면 도깨비가 출몰한다는 곳이었다. 지금은 근처까지 인가가 들어섰지만 옛날에는 해만 설핏하면 사람 발걸음이 끊기는 곳이었다. 그들은 거기서 자동차를 얻어 타기 위해서 기계적으로 손을 들었지만, 속으로는 옛날 고려적 비정한 관습을 새기고 있었다. 그 모퉁이는 산 부모 버리기가 없어진 다음에도 인적이 드문 귀기 어린 곳이었다. 그곳의 이름은 그들에게 무서운 곳의 대명사였다. 거기에 가자면 황토를 쌓아 땅 위에 길게 굴을 만들고 그 속에 진흙 기와, 진흙 벽돌들을 채곡채곡 쌓고 굴 입구를 장작더미로 막고 불을 처질러 높은 굴뚝으로 시커먼 연기를 토해내고 벽돌과 기와를 구워내는 벽돌공장 기와공장을 지났고, 그 다음에는 큰길에서 조금 들어가면 진흙을 빚어서 빙빙 돌려 모양새를 잡고 불에 구워 질그릇을 만드는 옹기공장이 있었다. 거기서 산 밑으로 더 들어가면, 그들은 거기까지 가본 적이 없었는데, 화장터가 있었고 그 뒤로 공동묘지가 있었다. 벽돌공장부터가 말하자면 고름장 모퉁이였다. 그들은 벽돌 기와공장을 지나 질그릇공장께에 와 있었다. 화장장

madness gleaming in their eyes from, no doubt, liquidating countless communist guerilla troops and conducting manhunts throughout the country. The star hopped in his private quarter-ton automobile with the canvas top replaced with black plywood and fled to Gwangju. It was truly that kind of time. The boys did not know whose gun it was that had turned up at school, or which student had brought it. That part didn't matter. What was important was that a student was carrying a gun at a school. Didn't matter which student, either—some other boy at school had a *gun*.

The school closed as soon as the war started. Their school had had some tough luck. At the end of World War II, the school—then a primary school which the boy had attended—was used as a barrack for Japanese soldiers fleeing from Manchuria. Meanwhile, the students studied at the mission center at the Catholic church next door. The boy used to look over the fence timidly, as though he was peeping in on a neighbor's house. The schoolyard was occupied by soldiers in shiny coats with long swords and fat horses.

In middle school, the boy's teachers had been conscripted into the South Korean army. The

의 둥글고 유난히 높은 굴뚝이 저만치서 눈에 들어왔다. 그들은 보통 때 같으면 올 일도 없고 오고 싶지도 않은 무서운 곳 한복판에 아무 두려움 없이 서서 도대체 무서운 곳이란 어떻게 생겼는가 찬찬히 살펴볼 수 있었다. 아무리 무시무시한 곳도 사람들만 많이 북적거리면 무서울 것이 없었다. 작고 붉은 민둥산과 높은 굴뚝 말고는 그들이 사는 시내 외곽의 딴 인적 없는 산천과 다를 것이 없었다. 똑같은 경치가 귀신 나오게 무서운 곳이 될 수 있는 것도 우스웠고, 또 그런 곳이 사람 조깨 많이 법석인다고 금방 오래된 풍속이 풍비박산하는 것도 얄궂은 일이었다. 사람들이 없어서 무서웠냐? 사람들이 있는 곳도 사람들만 떠나면 공포의 공간이 되냐?

"성, 사람을 태우면 흙이 되고, 흙을 태우면 집이 되냐?"

"흙을 어떻게 태우냐, 굽지?"

"오래 꾸면 탄디. 흙이 타면 숯이 되냐?"

"바보야, 숯은 나무가 탔어."

"재는 언제 되고?"

"숯이 탔어."

"한 번 타면 숯이고, 두 번 타면 재냐?"

"그래. 한꺼번에 재가 되기도 하고."

classes, desks, chairs and everything else in the former schoolhouse were moved to a large warehouse on the street in front of the East Primary. An upperclassman who had been slapped in the face by a history teacher sought revenge by using their school's new location against the teachers. Rather than reflecting on his actions as he was instructed to do, he threw a rock the size of a fist on the tin roof of the warehouse. The rock rolled off the side of the roof and made a thunderous sound like a stone wall tumbling down in the monsoon. The boys had been startled at first, but when they realized what the noise was, snickered to themselves while they studied the teacher's reactions. They were grateful for the interruption, and the old, pedantic, perfectionist teacher, who had been completely caught off guard by the unexpected incident, gave them an extracurricular joy they had never dared to dream of. When their school was left unoccupied for the night, they were instructed to come to the school together to guard their place of learning. They stood guard on school orders, but it was fun all the same.

They were used to being at school only when it was light out—it was different and exciting to be

"덜 타면 숯이고 다 타면 재냐?"

"그렇다니까. 숯은 굽는다."

"덜 타면 굽냐? 어찌 숯을 굽냐, 나무를 굽지?"

"나무가 생선이냐, 굽게?"

"고름장하면 고름이 나오냐? 고름이 나오면 고름장하
냐? 그래서 고름장이냐? 죽은 사람한테서도 고름이 나
오냐?"

"고름이 뭐이냐? 살 썩은 것이다. 산 사람은 곪은 데
만 고름이고, 죽은 사람은 온몸이 고름이다. 구더기들
은 즈그들 구미에 맞는 대로 송장 아무데서나 끓는다."

"구더기도 식성이 있냐? 먼저 썩은 데에 안 생기냐?
참, 썩기 잘했다. 안 썩었으면 얼마나 아프고 근지럽겠
냐? 한 군데 공곳만 곪아도 온몸에 열이 나는디."

"죽었는디 썩은 줄 아냐, 아픈 줄 아냐, 곪은 줄 아냐,
끓는 줄 아냐?"

"죽은 다음에 고름장 하냐? 살았을 때 안 하냐? 숨이
끊어질 때까지 사흘이고, 이레고, 보름이고, 얼마나 온
몸이 어수선허겄냐?"

"사람이 한꺼번에 죽냐? 조금씩 죽는다. 죽을 때가 되
면 안 죽어도 거의 죽었다. 팔다리에 힘 빠지면 상투 끝

there at night with the electric lights on. A certain mysterious spookiness lurking in the dark stirred their sense of adventure. The boy volunteered for school night watch as well. Any household without men had to pay or send the women out to do their part. One could also pay someone else to take their shift.

The boy often stood watch at night, sometimes for fun, other times for money. All he had to do was deliver messages between the guards above and below him by shouting the messages. The message was ususally: All clear. Pass it on. Nothing to it.

A few sleepless nights meant a new book for school. He bought an English grammar book. He had an English dictionary but no Korean dictionary, and while it had never occurred to him to buy a Korean grammar book, he had had his heart set on an English grammar book for some time.

The book happened to have a red band on its cover. He was on his way home with the book tucked under his arm when a stranger noticed it and approached him. Hey, what book is that? Excuse me? It's an English grammar book. May I take a look? Why? You're studying a foreign language

이 먼저 가고, 머릿속이 텅 비어야 똥 된장을 몰라본다."

"그러면 져다 버려도 버린 줄을 모르냐?"

"알았으면 지게 위에 올라타냐, 타란다고?"

"버리는 줄 알았어도 힘없으면 할 수 없다."

"몸에 힘이 빠지는디 머릿속이 온전허냐? 늙어지면 어린애로 돌아간다 하더라만, 늙은 애가 어린애를 무슨 수로 당하겠냐? 한 남자가 제 에미를 지게에다 지고 와서, 에미에다 지게까지 둘 다 두고 가려 하자, 애비 따라 고름장에 구경 나온 어린 아들, 왜 지게를 버리느냐 도로 집에 가져가자, 그가 크면 다음에 또 그 지게를 쓸 날 온다. 남들 따라 에미 버린 젊은 남자 깜짝 놀라, 부끄럽고 기특해서 에미 도로 업고 가니, 어린 손자 말 한마디 늙은 할미 구했구나."

"아이고, 성도. 노인이라고 속조차 없을라고. 아들 지게 얻어 타고 깊은 산속 가는 노파, 아들 혼자 돌아올 때 길 잃을까 걱정돼서, 손을 뻗어 길가에다 나뭇가지 꺾었구나."

"우리가 차 타고 떠나면, 우리가 부모를 버렸냐, 부모가 우리를 버렸냐?"

"차 안 타도 우리들이 모진 목숨 건지자고, 부모형제

160

when you haven't even properly learned your own? Let me have a look. The stranger yanked it out of his hands before the boy could stop him. He leafed through the book and read a few pages, and tossed it back to him in a suddenly cold, unfriendly manner. The boy was so moved that an ignorant man had taken an interest in his English grammar book that he didn't realize his hard-earned book had come close to being confiscated in the middle of the street in broad daylight.

News of impending war was no news or surprise to the villagers. They had lived in a state of war their entire lives. No. Not a state of war. "Turmoil" was more accurate. Turmoil was refugees endlessly pouring into town. Whether or not they heard rumors that you had to get to Palgeumsan to survive, whether or not they believed it, countless refugees continued their journey east toward the temporary capital.

The boy's family also packed up to flee. Everyone was packing up, but only the well-off could afford to go. After a long period of deliberation, his father concluded, in spite of his mother's opposition, that he and the boy's mother would stay while the boy and his brother would flee to Palgeumsan. He be-

사지에다 헌신처럼 내버렸다."

"차 안 서기 다행이다. 없는 틈을 비집 뚫고 달리는 차 매달리면, 하동 진주 천릿길을 언제 다시 돌아올꼬."

"여기서 무한정 기다리기 잘했다. 차 없어서 못 가는 것 우리 잘못 아닐 테지."

"아침나절 나간 형제 해 다 져서 끼대오면, 깐깐하신 울 아부지 또 얼마나 화내실까."

"생목이 아니라 광양에 갔다고 거짓말 꾸미자."

"생목이라니, 누구 다리 몽댕이 부러지는 꼴 볼라고? 섬진포구 진상까지 갔다고 둘러대면 너무 머냐?"

"입에 침이 아니라 바짓가랭이에 흙먼지나 묻히고."

"그래, 옷이 너무 깨끗허다."

"진상이면 하동 다 가고 전라 경상 어간인디, 거기까지 갔다가 빙충맞게 돌아왔다고 더 혼나면 어쩐다냐?"

"광양으로 하자. 광양도 시내가 아니라, 거기 다 가서 산소로 들어가는, 거 무슨 재냐, 그 재까지로 하자."

"그래. 광양 산소가 얼마나 머냐? 거기까지만 갔다 와도 우리 할 일은 다했다. 미련허게 돌아올 길 너무 멀리 갔다고 했으면 했지, 가라는 길 안 갔다고는 못 허실 테지."

그들은 어두워질 때까지 기다렸다. 여전히 지나가는

lieved that if they could not all evacuate, at least half of them should have a fighting chance at survival.

But even the fleeing half could not afford to leave. The boy and his older brother were too young to know better or to dare to go against their father's orders. They left as though they were leaving for a picnic—no dramatic protests about leaving their parents behind to die, not a single tear shed. The boys each carried a knapsack that contained food, clothes, and a wad of money. The circumstances were too peaceful for a perilous journey, but the reason for departure was too morbid for an excursion. The boy was neither scared nor excited. His boyhood curiosity was too blind to reality to inspire any real fear in him, while the unforeseeable future in both his village and where they were headed dampened his excitement. Remaining at home was as risky a gamble as leaving. Perhaps it was riskier. Being on the road could be a thrilling adventure for a boy sick and tired of hiding out in the comfort of his home. Escaping the everyday was a peril. His home was now in an emergency state. To leave home was to escape peril. It was to escape one peril and enter another.

차들에게는 손을 들었다. 세워달라는 것인지, 잘 가라는 것인지, 그들도 알 수 없었다. 사실 그것은 그들의 마음과는 상관없었다. 멈추면 세워달라는 신호였고, 그냥 내빼면 잘 가라는 인사였다. 그들의 마음은 편했다. 혹시 세워줄까봐서 걱정할 필요는 없었다.

"차가 서면 어쩔거냐?"

"타야지 뭐. 그런 염려 하들 말어. 한두 대 겪었어?"

"탈라면 안 서도, 안 탈라면 잘 선다. 눈먼 차가 꼭 있거든. 저기 봐라."

"어디? 정말! 차가 서네. 웬일이냐?"

그들은 그들을 지나서 멈춘 짐차를 향해서 뛰었다. 그들이 차에 도착하자 그들을 환영이라도 해야겠다는 듯이 사람들이 짐칸이고 차칸에서 꾸역꾸역 내렸다. 막상 그들이 멈춰 서자, 그 사람들은 흰자위를 번득이며 그들을 냉담하게 곁눈질했다. 환영이 아니었다. 환영은커녕, 바로 바라보아주지도 않았다. 그들은 형제를 알은 체할 여유가 없었다. 십 리도 못 가서 발병이 났다. 십 리라니, 문턱도 채 못 넘어서 발통에 바람이 샜다.

"이거 고칠라면 얼마나 걸리냐?" 앞 칸에서 내린 신수가 훤한 신사가 기름때 묻은 옷을 입은 운전수에게 물

It was to escape a grave peril for a lighter one, to circumvent the peril of life and death in a battlefield in favor of a life on the streets as wandering angels. Even without the guilt of abandoning their parents, even for fearless boys seeking adventure, leaving seemed cowardly. They left with heavy hearts.

Where the road divided to southbound and eastbound, and the eastbound road intersected with the railroad, the boy ran into his English teacher.

"I'll see you if we both come out of this alive, huh?" he said, grabbing the boy's hand with his own tremendous hands. He received his pupil's farewell and swiftly disappeared into the crowd. The boy remembered schoolmates who had been slapped by this teacher. They had complained of his large hands and exceptionally painful slaps. Once, the teacher came to class with rubber shoes and no socks. The students saw the dirt between his toes. Rubber shoes did not breathe much, so grime formed even on the cleanest feet. The teacher had the appearance of a country manservant or a woodsman. The boy knew that the teacher was an honest, hardworking, confident professional who adhered to his principles. The boy and his schoolmates could revel in poking fun at the

었다.

"얼마 걸리냐가 아니라, 때울 수 있을랑가 모르겠소. 동밖에 차부에 가야 때우는디, 그 사람들이라고 피난 안 가고 넘의 차 발통이나 때와주고 있겠소?"

"즈그들이 피난 가기는 어디로 가? 얼렁 빼갖고 가서 때와 와."

운전수는 벌써 차 앞축 밑에 솟을받침을 밀어 넣고 지렛대로 터진 바퀴를 들어올리고 있었다. 풍신 좋은 늙은 신사는 남문치과 원장이었다. 그는 그 지역 유지로, 그들이 다니는 학교의 후원회 회장이었다. 어른이야 자라나는 아이들이라 그들을 잘 몰라볼지 몰랐지만, 그들은 그들의 아버지의 친구인 그를 못 알아볼 수가 없었다. 그는 인사하기에는 너무 멀고, 모른 체하기에는 너무 가까워서, 그들에게는 어려운 인물이었다. 원장의 자제들도 그들에게는 알 듯 말 듯했다. 그들은 달려온 것을 후회했다. 더구나 태워달라고 사정하려고 온 것이 너무 속상했다. 저쪽에서도 냉대는 하지만 이쪽이 낮에 익은 눈치였다. 좁은 바닥에서 낯설지 않은 것이 얼마나 대수로울까마는, 그것이 양쪽을 더 불편하게 만들었다. 그들은 진퇴양난이었다. 다행히 치과원장이 차

teacher because they assumed the teacher would always be around to teach them English. Only when the teacher vanished in a cloud of dust did the boy realize how important the teacher had been to them. The thought of not being able to learn English from him again tugged at the boy's heart more so than the life and death situation he faced at that moment. The boy never did see this English teacher again, but he heard rumors years later that the teacher had returned to his home-town and had become head of the township.

They crossed the railroad and joined the other refugees. They waved every time a car went by to hitch a ride, but none stopped. They walked to Saengmok. According to their grandmother's tales, that place was a Goreumjang bend long ago. Sons brought their old parents on A-frame carriers to abandon them here. She said that tigers had been spotted here during the day and forest spirits appeared on drizzly nights. There were houses built nearby now, but in the past it used to be completely deserted by nightfall. They stood at the bend and waved absentmindedly as they thought about the merciless custom of old Goryeo.

The corner where the boys stood was a desert-

가 고장 난 것에 너무 화가 나서 근처에 웬 소년들 둘이
서 있는 것에는 미처 신경을 쓸 겨를이 없었다. 어쨌든
그들은 누구나 다니는 길 위에 서 있었고, 그들의 차는
순전히 우연히 거기에 멈췄다. 체면이나 안면이나 지면
같은 것은 한가할 때 천천히 챙겨도 늦지 않았다. 목숨
이 왔다 갔다 할 때는 딴 것들은 가만 내버려둬도 저절
로 제 앞들을 닦았다. 그는 소년들을 보면서도 그들이
거기 있는 것을 까맣게 몰랐다. 그들의 인사를 받을 준
비는 더욱 안 되었다. 인사란 서로 주고받는 것이어서
받을 사람한테만 했다. 어른의 냉담과 무심은 아이들에
게 자신과 용기를 주었다. 그들은 덕분에 조금도 죄 지
은 느낌 없이 홀가분하게 그 자리를 뜰 수 있었다. 남은
것은 뒤도 안 돌아보고 걸음을 걷는 일뿐이었다. 걷는
것은 쉬웠다. 발만 떼놓으면 되었다. 그들이 막 걸음을
옮기려 했을 때, 운전수가 투덜대며 욕하는 소리가 들
려왔다.

　"이런 제미럴 놈의 낫도가 꼼짝을 않네."

　들어 올려진 앞바퀴가 헛돌았다. 운전수가 바퀴를 차
에 고정하는 암놈 조임쇠를 풀려고 연장에 힘을 주면
그 힘이 고스란히 허공에 뜬 바퀴를 돌리는 데로 가버

ed, haunted place even after people had stopped leaving their parents there. The place symbolized fear to them. To get there, they had to pass the brick and roof tile factory where clay tiles and bricks were piled in long caves made of red clay that were sealed with a piles of wood. Black smoke poured out of the factory chimney as the bricks and tiles were fired. Farther in from the main street was the pottery factory where potters shaped clay on wheels and then fired them to make earthenware. Even farther down the mountain path—the boys had never been that far—was the crematorium, and behind that, the cemetery. But the Gore-umjang bend began at the brick factory.

They had passed the brick factory and were passing the earthenware factory. The unusually tall, cylindrical chimney of the crematorium came into view. They stood fearlessly in the middle of a place that they had long been afraid of and had had no occasion to visit. They took their time inspecting this ghoulish place for themselves. No matter how frightening a place, there was nothing to fear as long as it teemed with people. Apart from the barren red hill and the tall chimney, this place was no different from any other nature scene in the out-

려서 그는 힘을 쓸 수가 없었다. 수놈 조임쇠들과 암놈 조임쇠들이 벌겋게 녹이 슬어서 거의 한 몸들이 되었다. 보통 때 같으면, 여섯모꼴 암놈에 돌리개 연장을 밀착하고 바퀴가 돌아갈 틈이 없도록 시침을 떼고 있다가 느닷없이 연장을 홱 돌리면, 두어 번째에는 틀림없이 제아무리 어른 몸무게를 연장에 싣고 내리눌러 단단히 조인 암놈도 뚝 소리를 내고는 실없이 푸실푸실 풀어졌다. 성질 급한 운전수는 차 녹슨 것 생각 않고, 조임쇠가 고분고분 않은 것만 탓을 했다. 전문가의 손을 몰라보다니. 고집은 고철에만 있는 것이 아니라 고수에게도 있었다. 그는 이마에 땀방울을 송올송올 맺으면서 연방 힘을 쓰고 연방 욕을 뱉어냈다. 뭣 할 놈의. 뭣같이. 점잖은 사람이 안팎으로 위아래로 식구를 거느린 자리에서 옆 사람이 듣기에도 민망했다.

유지는 속수무책이었다. 바퀴 빼는 것을 그만두라고 하기 전에는 기술자의 험구를 막을 수 없었다. 그의 상소리는 거의 그의 힘든 일에 장단가락이었다. 상놈이 이럴 때 아니면 언제 양반 욕보이냐? 운전수는 그의 입에서 무슨 말이 나오는지 그도 모르는 사이에, 전혀 순진한 얼굴로, 역성혁명을 외쳤다. 아무나 피난을 갈 수

170

skirts of the city. It was absurd that a place like any other could be so frightening, and bizarre that a reputation for horror could be shattered so quickly by a small bustling crowd. Was it frightening because it was unpopulated? Do populated areas become a place of horror if deserted?

"Brother. If you burn a body, it turns into earth. If you burn earth, it becomes a house. Right?"

"You can't burn earth. You fire it."

"If you fire it long enough, it burns. If earth burns long enough, does it become charcoal?"

"Charcoal is burned wood, idiot."

"When does it become ash?"

"When the charcoal burns."

"Burn it once, you get charcoal. Burn it twice, you get ash?"

"Yes. Or it goes straight from wood to ash."

"You get charcoal if you burn it halfway, and ash if you burn it all the way?"

"Yes. And you *fire* charcoal."

"If you burn it halfway, you call it *firing*? And you fire the wood, not the charcoal."

"You can't fire wood. Wood doesn't work for you."

"Do you get gore if you practice Goreumjang? Is

없다고 생각한 원장이 불평등사회를 현실적으로 인정했다면, 반드시 그것에 대한 반발은 아니지만, 운전수가 모든 사람들에게 공통되는 것을 가식 없고 감춤 없는 말로 무심결에 되풀이하는 것은 계급타파, 사해동포의 강조 아닌 강조였다. 원장은 뒷짐을 지고 입맛을 다셨다. 팔금산을 그만둘 수도 없고, 가자니 길이 너무 멀고 험했다. 이런 고장이 이번 한 번으로 그치리라는 보장이 없었다, 한 번도 견디기가 딱 한 번이 너무 많다 싶은데. 운전수는 지나는 차들한테 도움을 청하고 싶은 마음이 없어 보였고, 차들도 도움을 청하더라도 응해줄 것 같지 않은 기세로 그들을 지나쳤다.

두 나이 어린 나그네들의 난데없는 나타남은 그 둘을 포함한 그곳에 있는 모든 사람들에게 까맣게 잊혀졌다. 운전수가 힘이라기보다는 꾀를 내기 위해서 잠시 일손을 놓고 옷 소맷자락으로 이마의 땀을 닦았을 때, 잊혀진 나그네들 중 하나가 당돌하게 앞으로 썩 나섰다. 그들은 뒤로 슬그머니 빠져나가기보다는 현장 한복판으로 뛰어드는 것이 더 쉬웠다. 슬며시 사라지는 데에는 때를 잡기가 힘들었지만, 톡 볼가지는 데에는 때가 없었다.

it Goreumjang if you get gore? Is that why they call it Goreumjang? It is gore if the person's already dead?"

"What's gore? Gore's blood that's been shed. For the living, gore is only spilled blood. For the dead, their entire body is gore. Maggots start eating wherever whets their appetite."

"Maggots don't have taste. They go wherever decomposition begins. Good thing they go at decomposed things, too. Just imagine how painful and itchy it would be if they didn't. An infection on a boil is enough to make you feverish all over."

"How would you know what's rotting, hurting, oozing, or being eaten when you're dead?"

"Do you do Goreumjang after you're dead? You do it when you're still alive. Imagine how awful your body must feel for however long it takes to die—three, seven days? A fortnight?"

"People don't die all at once. They die little by little. When it's time to die, they're still alive but as good as dead. When they lose control of their arms and legs, they start to lose their heads. And then when they completely lose their minds, they can't tell right from left."

"Then they can't tell they've been brought out and

"아저씨, 이것을 내려요." 그가 차 몸통을 괴고 있는 솟을받침에 꽂힌 작대기를 붙잡으며 말했다. 치과의사는 맹랑한 일도 다 있다는 눈초리로 그를 쳐다보았지만, 기술자는 그의 말에 그의 생각을 문득 깨달았는지 그의 어린 것을 탓하지 않고 순순히 솟을받침에 마치 마법의 코지름이라도 바르는 것처럼 잠깐 손을 댔다. 그가 기다렸다가 조금 전에 운전수가 했던 것과 똑같이 그 막대기를 위 아래로 꺼떡꺼떡 흔들었다. 차가 아까 와는 반대로 내려앉았다. 바퀴가 땅에 닿자 그는 움직임을 멈췄다. 그리고 운전수에게 자리를 내줬다. 운전수는 이번에는 마음껏 용을 쓸 수 있었다. 힘이 조금도 바퀴를 헛돌게 하는 데로 새지 않았다. 바퀴를 헛돌리자면 차의 무게보다 더 큰 힘이 필요했다. 운전수에게 그런 힘이 있지도 않으려니와, 아무리 녹슨 고물이라고 암수 조임쇠들이 그 큰 힘을 버틸 만큼 찰떡궁합으로 달라붙었을 리도 없었다. 조임쇠들은 약간의 저항을 한 뒤에 아까보다 못한 힘에도 줄줄이 풀렸다. 보고 있던 사람들이 냉대와 경계의 눈초리를 찬탄과 감사의 눈빛으로 바꿨다. 그들 사이에서 안도의 한숨이 거의 들리는 듯했다. 노련한 늙은 남자는 달랐다. 그는 경망되이

abandoned?"

"If they knew, you couldn't force them onto the A-frame carrier."

"Even if they knew, they wouldn't have any choice if they have no strength left."

"The mind leaks as the limbs grow weak. They say you become an infant again when you get old. An elderly child cannot take care of a young child. A man carried his mother away in an A-frame carrier to abandon her in the woods, A-frame carrier and all. But his young son who'd come along stopped his father and said, "Let's take the A-frame home, dear Father. For I might need it to carry you here some day." The man, ashamed of himself and proud of his son, took his old mother back to the house. Thus the old woman was saved thanks to the wit of her young grandson."

"Oh, Brother. Old people have decency and dignity. An old woman is carried deep into the woods on her son's A-frame carrier. Concerned her son will lose his way back to the village, she reaches out and snaps the branches to mark the path and take him to safety."

"We haven't hitched a ride yet, but look how we're running away, abandoning our parents in the bow-

표정을 바꾸지 않았다. 운전수가 차바퀴를 뽑는 것은 당연한 일이었다. 고마워해야 한다면 그것은 그가 아니라 딴 사람이 알아서 할 일이었다.

"서둘러. 지금 와도 늦었다."

심부름 떠나는 사람한테 오느냐고 묻는 격이었다. 그는 그 차가 아무래도 애깨나 태우겠고, 피난 갈 사람인지 아닌지는 사람이 아니라 그 고장 난 고물차가 결정할 것이라고 늙은 신사한테 한마디 해주고 싶었지만, 참았다. 그 차가 그들을 태워주지도 않겠지만, 그 차를 얻어 타자고 달려왔던 그들도 그 차를 포기한 지 오래였다. 어쩌면 달려오기 전에 이미 포기했었다. 그들은 마치 그 차의 고장을 고치는 것을 도와주려고 오기라도 했던 것처럼, 올 때보다 조금 더 떳떳해져서 그들을 떠났다.

"제일 큰일이 남았다." 그들이 아까 종일 서서 발들을 동동 구르던 자리께로 돌아왔을 때 고일인 형이 말했다.

"무슨 일?"

"집에 들어가는 일."

중이인 아우가 근심스럽게 고개를 끄덕거렸다.

els of hell to save our own miserable lives!"

"Good thing the cars won't stop. If we hop on a car that squeezes through the crowd, how on earth will we return the thousand *li* from Hadong and Jinju?"

"Good thing we waited here. If a car won't stop for us, it won't be our fault we couldn't run away."

"If the brothers who fled in the morning return home after dusk, our fussy father will be furious."

"Let's lie. Tell them we've been to Gwangyang and back, not Saengmok."

"They'll beat us half to death if they find out we only made it as far as Saengmok. Do you think it'll be too much if we said we made it to Chinsang at the inlet of Seomjin River and back?"

"And returned with our pants so clean?"

"You're right. We're too clean."

"Chinsang is near Hadong and almost on the border of Jeolla and Gyeongsang. We'll be scolded for coming all the way back from there like a couple of dimwits."

"How about we say Gwangyang? Not downtown, but that hill just before the cemetery. The hill— whatever it's called."

"Okay. The cemetery in Gwangyang is pretty far

화포 대포

    그들은 날이 저문 뒤에 집에 들어왔다. 그들을 맨 먼저 본 것은 그들의 어머니였다. 그들은 안심했다. 꾸중 안 듣는 것 정도는 기대할 수 있었다. 잘하면 환영을 받을지도 몰랐다. 그들은 어머니의 눈치를 살폈다. 냉랭했다. 우선 말이 없었다. 그들은 불길한 예감이 들었다. 혹시 그들이 돌아와서 화가 나셨을까? 그들은 그들의 고생을 과장했다. 어머니는 그들의 말에 별로 귀를 기울이지 않았다. 실제로 갔던 거리의 열 배를 갔다고 한 것 말고는 대개 사실이었다. 어머니는 그들의 수고에 전혀 동요하지 않았다. 그들은 입을 다물었다. 어머니는 그들이 돌아온 것에 화가 난 것이 아니라, 그들이 돌아올 길을 간 것에 화가 났다. 그들의 헛고생에 부아가 났고, 그들의 헛수고가 그것으로 끝나지 않은 것에 노여웠다. 어차피 피난길을 떠나야 한다면, 그들이 한 피난에 실패하고 돌아온 것은 조금도 즐거운 일이 아니었다. 싫은 일을 하지 못한 것이 하나도 기쁘지 않다니! 어머니는 어디로 피난을 가는 것에 반대가 아니라, 어디고 간에 도대체 피난을 떠나는 것에 불만이었다. 왜 도

away, isn't it? They'll think we've done our duty if we made it there and back. They might still say we stupidly went too far, but they can't accuse us of not going far enough."

They waited until dusk. They continued to wave at the cars. Whether they were waving them down or waving goodbye, even they themselves did not know. Perhaps it did not matter. It was a signal to stop the car if the car stopped, and a wave good-bye if it drove on. They felt at ease—no need to worry that one of the cars might stop for them.

"What should we do if one of them actually stops?"

"We hop on, I guess. Don't worry about that. You know how they are."

"They never stop when you want them to, but they do when you don't want them to. The odd car always does. Look!"

"Where? You're right! A car did stop. That's un-usual."

They ran toward the truck that went past them and stopped down the road. As they ran toward the truck, people poured out the back as though they were stepping off to welcome the boys. But when the boys arrived at the truck, the passengers'

망치냐? 무슨 죄를 지었냐? 감투를 썼냐, 떼돈을 벌었냐, 행세를 했냐, 넘 못할 짓을 했냐? 쳐들어오는 사람들은 조선 사람들 아니냐? 옛날에 되놈들, 왜놈들 겪었고, 근자에 왜놈들, 양놈들 견뎠다. 조선 사람이 조선 사람 못 참냐? 그들의 어머니는, 그들의 아버지가 이상주의인데 비하면, 현실주의였다. 그들의 아버지는 해방 후 혼란기에 사업을 한번 해보려고 잔뜩 벼르기만 했지, 실상 일에 손을 대지 못했다. 하는 일은 하려는 일의 시작이 아니라, 그것과는 상관없는 단순한 임시방편의 호구지책이었다. 그는 그가 하고 있는 일이 아니라 하려고 하는 일에 의해서 평가받기를 원했다. 하는 일에 의하면 그는 거의 무직자였다. 하는 일은 소꿉장난 같았고, 하려는 일은 벅찼다. 그는 현실과 이상 사이에서 헤매다가 지쳤다. 하나는 너무 추악했고, 또 하나는 너무 멀었다. 한번은 술에 취해서 그가 소리쳤다. 여름날 저녁, 밥을 먹고 식구들이 마당에 평상을 내놓고 앉아서 더위를 식히고 있을 때였을 것이다.

"나는 공산주의보다 더 무서운 무정부주의자다. 아냐?"

그들의 어머니가 질겁을 했다. 무정부주의가 무엇인지는 몰라도 공산주의라는 말이 무서웠다. 누가 들으면

regarded them coldly. The boys were not welcome. The passengers did not even meet the boys'
gaze. The passengers did not have the presence of
mind to acknowledge them. Scarcely ten *li* from
home, their feet could carry them no farther. No,
not even ten *li*. They were barely out of the village
when the truck got a flat tire.

"How long to get this fixed?" A striking gentleman
got out of the passenger seat and asked the driver
in oil-stained clothes.

"How long is not the problem. Not sure if this can
be patched at all. We need to take this truck to a
shop outside the village, but everyone's evacuating.
No one in the right mind will come back to fix
someone else's car."

"They got no place to go. Take the wheel off and
go get it patched. And make it quick."

The driver had already pushed the jack under the
front of the car and was lifting up the side of the
car. The handsome gentleman was the chief dentist
at Nammun Dental Clinic. He was an influential man
in the village and the head of the school support
foundation. He, perhaps, did not recognize the
boys as adults often do not recognize children who
change considerably as they grow. But it was diffi-

어쩔라고 저런다냐. 담 너머 사방이 넘의 집인디. 아마 난리가 끝난 훨씬 뒤의 일이었다. 어머니는 이념이 무엇인지 관심이 없었다. 새끼들하고 먹고사는 것이 급했다. 아버지도 처자식들 맥여살리려고 손가락 끝이 닳도록 일했지만, 하는 일을 그의 인생 전부로 받아들이기에는 현실이 너무 불만족이었다. 더러운 현실은 일시적이고 잠정적이고 우발적이고, 목적도 방향도 가치도 없었다. 그는 딴 데서 위안을 구했고, 그가 공산주의자들이 반동으로 지목하기에 충분한 잠재적 남한의 요인이라고 생각했다. 계획도 사업의 일부였다. 이상주의자가 이상주의인 공산주의를 피하자 하고, 현실주의자가 현실적 폭력인 전쟁을 무서워하지 않은 것은 시대의 반어였다. 피난 가자고 한 것은 그의 아버지였고, 그의 어머니는 왜 피난 가냐고 반대였다. 그의 어머니가 그의 아버지를 이길 수는 없었다. 이상주의자의 말은 현실주의자의 말 앞에서 항상 옳았다. 그들은 피난을 가기로 결정했다. 그의 아버지가 그의 어머니를 완전히 설득할수는 없었다. 현실이 이상보다 더 삶에 가까웠다. 난리를 피한다면 난리가 없는 곳으로 가야 했다. 그들의 집형편으로는 전쟁이 없을 곳으로 가족 모두가 가는 것은

cult for the boys to not recognize their father's friend. The boys did not know the denist well enough to acknowledge him, but they also felt uneasy about ignoring him altogether. The gentleman's children were likewise vague acquaintances to the boys. The boys wished they had not run after the truck. They were embarrassed that they had come to beg for a ride.

The gentleman maintained his cold gaze but seemed to be trying to place the boys. The village was small so it was hardly unusual to run into an acquaintance. These circumstances made both parties quite ill at ease. They could not advance nor retreat. Fortunately, the gentleman seemed to have decided he was far too irritated about the flat tire to worry about a pair of boys hanging around. After all, they were standing on a public road and the truck had just happened to stop there. Repute, acquaintance, and introductions could certainly be postponed for a more convenient time. When life hung by a thread, everything else had a way of working itself out. The gentleman saw the boys but did not realize they were there. He was not ready to accept their greetings. The boys meant to exchange greetings but only if the gentleman was

불가능했다. 모두는커녕 일부가 가는 것도 실패했다. 그렇다고 앉아서 죽음을 맞냐? 어차피 난리 속이라면 객지보다 고향이 낫다. 서서 죽는 것보다는 앉아 죽고 누워서 죽는 것이 더 편타. 전쟁 속이라고 다 같냐? 살육 없는 곳이 안 되면 피비린내가 덜 심한 곳을 찾아가자. 그런 데를 누가 아냐? 촌이 꼭 시내보다 더 안전하냐? 사람들이 많이 사는 데보다 적게 사는 데가 더 낫다. 아무도 안 사는 데면 더욱 좋냐? 사람이 없으면 싸움도 없냐? 아예 산속으로 들어가냐? 산에 들어가서 반란군이 되냐? 그때 산골 사람들이 왜 도시로 소개했냐? 그때는 산이 싸움터였다. 지금은 들판이냐? 지금은 전국이었다. 군인들이 산에 있을 때는 평야로 피난 가고, 군인들이 산에서 내려오면 산으로 피난 갔다. 군인들이라니, 그때, 산에는 공비, 들에는 국군이었다. 반란군이든 진압군이든, 총질만 안 하면 곁에 있어도 괜찮았다. 피난은 총 쏘는 군인들을 피했다. 총만 없으면 군인들도 괜찮냐? 군인들은 없으면 좋고, 있어도 총만 없으면 괜찮고, 총이 있어도 안 쏘면 해가 없고, 총을 쏘아도 사람을 안 죽이면 옆에 있어도 무방했다. 그런 군대가 세상에 어디 있냐? 차라리 없기가 쉽지. 총 없는 군대가

184

willing to accept them. The adult's coldness and indifference gave the children confidence and courage to take off without the slightest bit of lingering guilt. All that was left to do was to walk away and not look back. Walking was easy. One foot ahead of the other. Just as they were about to take their first step, the driver swore and complained.

"The motherfucking nut won't budge."

The raised wheel kept turning with the nut. Each time the driver tried to loosen the lug nut by turning the iron, the force turned the wheel instead. The nuts were rusted red and nearly welded to the bolts. You could generally slip the head of the iron over the bolt, catch the bolt unawares by turning it abruptly, and the nut would come loose with a metallic crack. Even tightly screwed nuts like these had to yield after two or three tries with the weight of a full grown man on them. Eventually the pressure on the lug nuts would have to slacken under the iron. The impatient driver blamed the unyielding nuts rather than the rusty car. How dare it refuse the touch of an expert! The mechanical expert turned out to be as stubborn as the nut.

Sweat beaded his forehead as he alternated between cursing and going at the wheel. Something

어디 있고, 총이 있는데 안 쏘며, 총을 쏘는데 사람 안 다치냐? 사격장에서 총 아무리 쏘아도 사람 안 죽었다. 총 멘 군인들보다 맨몸 군인들이 더 많을 때도 있었다. 그럴 때는 평화였다. 아예 군인들이 안 보여도 이상해 할 사람 하나 없었다. 그들은 눈에 안 띄는 것이 정상이 었다. 평화가 정상인지 전쟁이 정상인지 알 수 없지만, 사람 살상 안 하는 총알, 불을 안 뿜는 총, 총 없는 군인, 군인 없는 세상이 어디 있냐? 그런 세상이 좋은 세상인 줄은 알겠다만, 그것이 정상일 리는 없었다. 동서고금 에 그런 세상이 없었다. 없는 세상을 정상이라고 우기 면 뭘 하냐? 있는 세상, 그것도 많이 있는 세상이 정상 아니냐? 인류 역사는 전쟁의 역사라더라. 세상이 군대 를 마다하고 군대가 전쟁을 싫어하느니, 차라리 멤생이 보고 물똥을 싸라고 해라. 하제를 멕여라. 군인들은 전 쟁을 싫어했다. 군대만큼 그것을 무서워하는 집단도 없 었다. 군대는 그것을 알았다. 군인들은 모든 수단을 써 서 그것을 막았다. 그들은 참호를 파고, 진지를 짓고, 돌 탑을 올렸다. 금성탕지, 그것도 부족해서 철조망을 치 고 그 바깥에 지뢰들을 묻었다. 그들은 서로 부딪히지 않는 한 절대 싸우지 않았다. 부딪혀도 생명이 위험해

son of a something something. It was awkward even for those looking on—a gentleman, his family and friends, the elderly, and the children watching as profanity spewed out of the driver's mouth. The gentleman was powerless. He could not silence the technician unless he was willing to give up on the tire. Foul language was like a work song for the driver. And, after all, he had to savor an opportunity for a drudge like him to humiliate a gentleman. Without realizing what he was saying, the driver as good as shouted, "All hail the revolution!" He had an innocent expression on his face. While the gentleman effectively accepted social inequality by implying that not everyone could afford to flee from the war, the driver—without meaning to—had purported a brotherhood of mankind and the end of class divisions by absentmindedly chanting words that stood for the simple, honest common denominator that bound them all. The gentleman smacked his lips, his hands behind his back. He could not give up on Palgeumsan but the road ahead seemed too long and difficult. There was no guarantee that this would be the last car failure. One failure was one too many. It did not appear that the driver was willing to accept assistance from passers-by who

야 싸웠다. 그것이 전쟁을 좋아하는 것이냐? 목숨이 위태로우면 미물도 독을 뿜었다. 뱀 봐라. 안 밟으면 안 물었다. 막대기 하나가 무서운데, 뱀이 사람을 보면 산이 움직이는 것 같을 것이다. 얼마나 겁나겠냐? 그래도 안 물었다. 안 건드리면 힐끗힐끗 돌아보고 혀를 날름거리면서 욕을 하고 제 갈 길을 갔다. 아마 욕도 아닐 것이다. 혼자 중얼거리지도 못하냐? 괴뢰군이 쳐들어와서 부딪혔나? 어떤 허수아비? 북괴군하고 국군이 됐건, 인민군하고 국방군이 됐건, 같으니까 싸운다. 같다니, 인민군하고 국군이 어찌 같냐? 자유수호하고 적화야욕하고 어찌 같냐? 정반대 아니냐? 군인이 군인하고 안 같으면 누하고 같냐? 모든 군인들은 같았다. 모든 전쟁들은 같은 전쟁들이었다. 피아 따지지 마라. 피난은 군대가 없는 곳, 총이 없는 곳, 총을 쏘지 않는 곳, 총이 잘 맞지 않는 곳으로 갔다. 하필 팔금산이냐. 임시수도는 커녕, 텅 빈 빌 공자 팔공산이면 어떠냐? 조선 천지 어디 가면 공산명월 없겠냐. 군대가 구름 같고, 총포가 충천하고, 총질이 난도질이라, 할 수 있냐, 쏘아도 맞지 않고 맞아도 덜 아픈 곳으로 가자. 그런 곳이 어디냐? 촌이었다. 왜 촌이냐? 촌에는 사람보다 자연이 더 많았다.

zipped by with a speed and passion that clearly demonstrated their reluctance to help.

The sudden appearance of the two young way-farers had been entirely forgotten by all present, including by the boys themselves. While the driver put his tool down for a moment to come up with an alternate plan and wipe his forehead with his sleeve, one of the forgotten wayfarers brazenly stepped in. It was easier for them to jump into the scene than to slip away; finding the right timing for a quick exit was tricky, but any time was a good time to make an entrance.

"Sir, crank this down," he said, grabbing the lever in the jack. The gentleman looked up and down at the boy as though he had never seen anything so insolent, but the technician seemed to know what the boy was suggesting. Instead of scolding the boy, he gently placed his hand on the lever as though he was putting a spell on it. The boy gave him a moment and then stepped up to the tire to pump the lever up and down as the driver had done earlier. The car lowered. The boy stopped when the tire reached the ground, and then he let the driver reclaim his place. The driver could goad the nut as much as he wanted without the tire

도시는 그 반대였다. 자연보다 사람이 더 많았다. 총이 무엇이냐? 사람이 만든 것이었다. 사람의 소작이 사람들 속에서 행세를 했지, 신의 소작 앞에서는 힘을 쓸 수 없었다.

그들은 남쪽으로 피난을 갔다. 정확히 말하자면 남서쪽이었다. 북쪽에서 쳐들어오는 군대는 아직 들이닥치지 않았고, 남동쪽으로 달아나는 군대는 이미 꼬리를 감춘 뒤였다. 군사적으로만 말하자면 무주공산, 아니 무주강산이었다. 달라진 것은 아무것도 없었다. 있으나 마나한 것, 없어도 전혀 없는 것 같지 않은 것은 없는 것이 더 좋았다. 그것은 그 물건의 유기적 부분이 아니었다. 불필요하고, 재수 없으면 해로운, 말하자면 암과 같은 존재였다. 그들은 그릇들을 땅에 묻고, 남부여대, 우선 먹고살 것들을 나눠서 이고 지고, 길을 떠났다. 이십 리를 가자 그들의 가까운 조상들이 묻힌 산소의 입구가 나왔다. 그들은 선산 앞을 지났다. 그곳은 그들이 수없이 갔던 어느 때와도 같이 평화로웠다. 군인들은 물론, 그들 말고는 피난민들도 없었다. 달라진 것은 아무것도 없었다. 있다면 바로 그들이었다. 군인들과 난민들을 예상하는 그들의 기대였다. 그 생각은 그곳에 깃든 정

turning. To loosen the bolt, one needed force greater than the weight of the truck. The driver was, of course, not that strong and the nuts and bolts could not possibly have been so fused together that they could withstand the weight of the car. The nuts resisted for a moment but loosened quickly with little effort. The cold vigilance of the bystanders turned to admiration and gratitude. One could almost hear the sigh of relief among all of them. All except the gentleman, of course. He did not alter his expression lightly. The driver was only doing his duty in removing the wheel; it was not the master's duty to be grateful to his servant.

"Hurry. We'd still be delayed if you returned with the patched tire this very minute." It was like telling a servant setting out on an errand to come back this instant. The boy wanted to tell the gentleman that the truck was likely to cause quite a bit of trouble, and that this broken lemon—not he—would decide who was to flee or not. But he kept it to himself. The truck would not give them a ride, but the boys who had run after the truck had long given up on it. Perhaps they had given up before they had begun running. As if they had come up with no alternative than to fix the car, they returned

적을 살벌하게 만들고도 남았다. 그곳을 도망쳐야 할 곳으로 만드는 것은 그곳을 도망치고 있는 그들 자신이었다. 거기서 그들은 큰길을 버리고 논길로 들어서서 십 리를 더 갔다. 그의 귀에 익은 이름의 동네들을 지났다. 그는 그때까지 그 동네들에 온 적이 없었다. 그 동네들에서 온 학생들이 그의 반에 더러 있었다. 이름만 알고 물건을 모르다가 그 물건을 만났을 때 드러나는 그 둘 사이의 큰 차이가 주는 놀라움이 부르트도록 지친 그의 발에 잠깐씩 휴식을 주었다. 물건의 모습은 이름만 들었을 때 생각했던 것과는 대개 언제나 달랐다.

그것은 이름이 나타내는 것보다 더 크고 복잡했다. 대체로 더 더럽고 너절했지만, 이름 밖에 있는 것들이 너무 많아서 미처 그런 것을 알은체할 틈이 없었다. 놀라움은 잠깐, 곧 다시 다리가 아프고, 허리가 결리고, 어깨가 땡겼다. 큰길 이십 리보다 샛길 십 리가 훨씬 더 멀었다. 갈수록 풍경은 피난과는 거리가 멀었다. 피난민은 그들뿐이었다. 그들은 차츰 그들이 피난민들이라는 것을 잊었다. 그들이 지금 지나고 있는 곳은 피난 가는 곳이냐, 피난 나온 곳이냐? 가는 곳이라면, 그곳과 그들이 버리고 온 곳과 무엇이 다르며, 나온 곳이라면, 얼마를

a little more confident than when they had first come. As if they had come running after the truck for no other reason than to fix the car, they left a little more confident than when they came.

"Now, for the hardest part," said the tenth grader, the older brother, as they passed the spot they had stood to hitch a ride before the truck stopped.

"What?"

"Returning home."

The eighth grader nodded gravely.

Hwapo and Daepo

They returned after sunset. Their mother was the first to spot them. The boys were relieved. Surely they weren't in for a scolding. They might even be welcomed back. They studied their mother's reaction. Frigid. She had nothing to say. They began to feel nervous. Was she angry that they had returned? They exaggerated the trouble they had been through. Mother was not interested. Apart from stretching the distance they traveled tenfold, most of their account had been true. Mother was not in the least moved by their troubles. They shut

더 가야 난리 없는 땅이 나오냐? 그들이 사선을 넘었냐? 안 넘었냐? 안 넘었다. 사선이 뒤따라오냐? 얼마나 바짝 따라오냐? 무엇이 사선이냐? 두 군대들이 맞붙어 싸우는 데냐? 달아나는 군대를 쫓아가는 딴 군대의 맨 앞줄이냐? 그 줄이 해안선에 닿으면 그들은 바닷속으로 풍덩 뛰어드냐? 안 뛰어들면, 그 줄 안으로 들어가서 그 딴 군대와 한 통속이 되냐? 난리 한복판으로 피난을 가냐? 분명한 것은, 고향을 버리는 것이 피난이었다. 피난 가는 사람들이 사는 곳에서 피난 가지 않는 사람들이 사는 곳으로 가는 것이 피난이었다. 어디고 사람들이 술렁대지 않고 눌러앉아 사는 곳이면 피난처였다. 그들이 지나가고 있는 동네들이 그런 곳이었다. 그는 아무데고 멈출 수 있다고 생각했다. 빠를수록 좋았다. 집으로부터 더 멀어진다는 것 말고는 지친 발로 걷는 것이 아무 뜻이 없어 보였다. 아버지의 생각은 달랐다. 난리 때에는 집이 멀수록 좋았다. 난리를 피하는 것은 아는 사람들을 피하는 것이었다. 그들은 첨산 밑 한골의 한 아는 사람 집에서 점심을 먹었다. 거기에도 아는 사람들이 있었다.

뽈록산은 평지 돌산이었다. 높이는 얼마 안 되었지만

up. Mother was not upset that they had returned, but that they had to leave in the first place. She was furious over the futility of their trip, and livid that this would not be the end of their troubles. If they had to flee anyway, a failed attempt was no cause for celebration. Getting upset over not being able to do what she didn't even want to do in the first place! Mother hadn't taken issue with the destination of their flight. She took issue with the flight itself.

Why run away? What was their crime? Had they gained fame from the war? Suddenly come into money? Were they posers? Were they doing what others could not? Weren't the invaders also Koreans? They had suffered through the Chinese and the Japanese in the past, and the Japanese and the Americans in the more recent past. Koreans could handle fellow Koreans.

Their mother, unlike their idealistic father, was a realist. Upon liberation, their father concocted a number of wild business plans, none of which evolved past the idea. He was not actually starting a business but engaged in merely temporary means of making ends meet. He wanted to be judged not by the work he did but the work he intended to

멀리서 보기에 첨탑처럼 돌올한 산이었다. 그는 그때까지 그 산 밑에 와본 적이 없었다. 십 리 떨어진 그의 산소 입구에서 멀리 바라보기는 수없이 했다. 그 산은 그 동네의 구장영감에 의하면 그 일대의 진산이었다. 그 산꼭대기는 명당으로 소문이 났다.

"한발이 심하면 동네에서는 산꼭대기에서 기우제를 지냅지요. 산에 갈 때는 삽허고 곡괭이를 나눠 들고 갑넨다."

"연장은 왜요?"

"사람들이 밤중에 남의 눈을 피해서 몰래 암장을 합넨다. 거기다 묘를 쓰면 가뭄이 듭지요. 일인 발복에 만인 기근이지요."

"동네 물이 한 골로 몰리면 큰물 지겠소이다. 외지 사람이 시신을 지고 들어올까요?"

"속을 아는 인근 사람들이 무명필에 유골을 싸가지고 안고 와서 평장을 합지요."

"멀리서도 옵니다. 옛날 누루하치의 어머니가 처녀쩍에 호수에 사는 수중괴물이 처녀를 범해서 아들을 낳았는디, 그 아들이 성장하매 또 물가에서 매양 놀기를 좋아하는지라, 그 어미가 피는 못 속인다고 한탄하거늘,

do. As far as what he actually did, he was one rung above unemployed. What he actually did was nearly child's play, and what he aspired to do was unmanageable. He grew weary in his blind search between reality and his ideals. One was too pitiful, and the other was unattainable.

Once, on a drunk rage, he'd shouted, "I am an anarchist! More terrifying than a communist, you know!"

It was a summer evening, and the family had been cooling off on the patio in the yard after dinner. Their mother was aghast. She did not know what an anarchist was, but the word "communist" scared her. What if someone had heard him? There were neighbors all around. This was long after the turmoil had passed. Mother had no interest in politics. Feeding her children was more pressing. Father also worked himself to the bone to feed his wife and kids. But the reality of his everyday life was too grim for his work to be the sum of his life. His grim reality was fleeting, provisional, and incidental, without purpose, direction, or worth. He sought solace in other things, and thought of himself as a potential key figure among South Korean reactionaries, worthy of communist apprehension.

어느 날 한 도인이 지나다가 물속의 구멍을 굽어보면서 찬탄해마지 않더니, 마침 물속에서 자맥질하고 있던 누루하치를 불러 품에 품고 있던 상자를 내주며 이르기를, 그것을 저 구멍 속에 깊숙이 넣어주면 그를 장차 후사하리라 하니……"

"어른들 말씀 중에 함부로 끼어드는 것 아니다."

"놔두시지요. 아이들 말이라고 중간에 끊는 법이 아닙지요. 허, 허."

"너무 길다. 짧게 해라."

"예. 누루하치가……."

"이미 길었다. 그만해."

"관둬. 성이 헐라고."

"내버려둬라. 이야기가 재미있다. 허, 허."

"어린 누루하치가 행인이 시키는 대로 상자를 맨 위 제왕혈에다 넣는 척하고 그 아래 부귀혈에다 넣고는, 집에 가서 그 어미한테 죽은 아비의 유골 묻힌 데를 물어 물가에서 뼈를 찾아 제왕혈에다 묻었더니, 미구에 그 소년이 나라를 일으키고 황제가 되었답니다."

"눈치도 없이."

"왜 그래? 짧게 요약했는디."

The plan for evacuation was part of his business. It was a great irony of the times that an idealist evaded the idealistic philosophy of communism and the realist was unperturbed by the real violence of war.

Father suggested evacuation and Mother saw no reason for it. Mother could not win an argument with Father. Idealism was always right when pitted against reality. They agreed to evacuate. But Father could not completely convince Mother. Reality was closer to life than ideals. To escape turmoil, you had to go where there was none. But they did not have the funds to deliver the entire family to a place safe from war. Even the half they sent away returned unsuccessful. So were they just supposed to sit around waiting for death to come? Dying at home is better than dying in some faraway place if we can't avoid mayhem. It's more comfortable to die sitting or lying down than on your feet. War is not the same everywhere. If we can't find any place safe from slaughter, we'll go some place with less of it. Who knows where that might be? Is the countryside really safer than the cities? The less populated areas are better. So an unpopulated area would be best? Is there no fighting if there aren't any people living there? So do we go into the

그들은 마당에다 덕석을 깔고 둥근상에 밥을 먹었다. 산나물들에 푸성귀 겉절이에 계란찜에 된장국에 하얀 쌀밥이었다. 먹거리들이야 노상 먹던 것들이었지만 솜씨가 달라서 맛이 입에 설었다. 별로 손 탈 것이 없는 밥도 맛이 달랐다. 우선 양이 엄청나게 많았다. 어린 그들 앞에 놓인 유기그릇에는 밥이 밑으로 한 그릇 위로 한 그릇, 거의 두 그릇이 담겨 있었다. 그것은 장정의 밥그릇이었다. 배가 고파서 구미가 당기기도 했지만, 어른 대접을 받는 것이 기분 좋았다. 그들은 어른들보다 더 빨리 밥그릇을 비웠다. 하얀 바지저고리를 입은 주인 남자는 농부라기보다는 선비 같아 보였다. 유색 치마저고리를 입은 주인 여자는 주인이라기보다는 일하러 온 동네 여자 같아 보였다. 생김새도 남자는 잘나고 여자는 못생겼지만, 처세가 더 그랬다. 그녀는 몸피도 작고 얼굴도 조막만했는데, 남 앞에 나서기를 싫어했다. 궂은일은 도맡아 하면서도, 얼굴을 내려 하지 않았다. 남자는 그의 아버지와 겸상으로 점심을 먹었지만, 그녀는 그들과 함께 먹지 않고 아마 부엌에서 남들 다 먹고 난 다음에 밥시중 다 들고 나서 먹는 둥 마는 둥 하는 눈치였다. 말하자면, 남자는 그 집 한량이었고, 여자는 그 집

mountains? Do we go into the mountains and join the guerrilla army? So why were the people in the mountains relocated to the city? The war was in the mountains? And now it has moved to the fields? Now it's all over the country. When the soldiers were in the mountains, people evacuated to the fields, and when the soldiers came down to the fields, people went back up into the mountains. Soldiers? The ones in the mountains are communist guerrillas and the fields are occupied by the ROK army. Doesn't matter if the area was occupied by guerrillas or the suppressing forces as long as they don't open fire. Fleeing means getting away from soldiers who shoot. So soldiers are okay as long as they don't shoot? We can do without soldiers, but they're okay as long as they don't have guns, and guns're okay as long as the soldiers don't use them, and shooting's okay as long as the bullets don't kill anyone. No army in the world is like that. There are no armies without guns, and soldiers with guns will always shoot, and shooting leads to injury. You can shoot all you want at the shooting range without killing anyone. Sometimes there were more soldiers without guns than ones with guns. Things were peaceful then. No one

일꾼이었다. 집안일은 말할 것도 없이 그녀 몫이었고, 논농사는 모르지만 밭일도 아마 남자보다는 그녀가 상일꾼이었다. 그들보다 조금 더 어린 그 집 아들들 둘이 그녀의 치맛자락에 매달리는 것 말고는 그녀가 그 집에서 차지하고 있는 자리를 보여주는 것은 아무것도 없었다. 종처럼 일하는 것은 그들의 어머니와 비슷했고, 주인 노릇 한사코 안 하기는 그들의 어머니와 달랐다. 그들의 어머니는 둘 다 했다.

그는 그때까지 그의 어머니가 노예처럼 일한다고 생각한 적이 없었다. 그 집 여자가 집안일 하는 것을 보고 그것과 비슷한 그의 어머니의 일이 무엇과 같은지를 깨달았다. 종처럼 일하는 것이 결코 나빠 보이지 않았다. 종처럼이건 주인처럼이건, 일하는 것이 그때처럼 훌륭하고 아름다워 보인 적이 없었다. 일은 주인처럼이 아니라 종처럼 해야 일이었다. 감독이나 사치나 오만이나 나태는 종이 아니라 주인처럼 했다. 주인 일 따로, 종 일 따로였다. 둘 다 하면, 고역의 광채가 게으름의 그림자에 가려 빛을 잃었다. 고된 일 하기는 어려웠고, 편한 일 하기는 쉬웠다. 둘 다 하기가 어려웠지만, 노동이 하도 어려워서 그것 하나 하는 것이 둘 다 하는 것보다 더 훌

thought it strange if we went for days without seeing a single soldier. It was normal for them to stay out of sight. I don't know which is the norm, war or peace, but there's no such thing as a bullet that doesn't kill, guns that don't fire, soldiers without guns, and worlds without soldiers. I understand that a world like this would be a great world, but it's not normal. There has never been a place like that anywhere in the world, not since the beginning of history. There's no use insisting that a world that doesn't exist is normal. A world that exists and exists in abundance is the norm. People say the history of mankind is a history of warfare. Asking the world to disband their armies and wishing for armies against war is like expecting a goat to make watery shit. Feed them laxatives. Soldiers don't like wars. No group of people fears it more than armies do. The armies know this, and soldiers use all tactics at their disposal to make sure wars don't happen. They dig trenches, they set up camps, and make fortresses of stone. Castles of steel and moats filled with boiling water. They even put up barbed wire and bury landmines along the walls. They don't fight as long as there aren't any conflicts. Even if there are conflicts, they hold off

룽했다. 그 다음이 둘 다 잘하는 것이었다. 주인 노릇만 잘하는 것은 둘 다 못하는 것보다 더 나빴다. 즉 가장 나빴다. 그의 어머니는 첫 번째와 두 번째를 오락가락했다. 주로 두 번째였다. 전에 그는 첫 번째가 있는 줄 몰랐다. 두 번째를 첫 번째로 알았다. 그의 어머니가 하는 것이 첫 번쩬 줄 알았다. 그것보다 더 좋은 것이 있는 것이 분명해지자, 그의 어머니는 처음부터 첫 번째를 했고, 따라서 언제나 첫 번째를 했고, 그의 어머니가 첫 번째를 한다는 그의 생각은 예나 이제나 잘못된 것이 아니었다. 그의 어머니가 하는 것보다 더 좋은 것이 있다는 것을 몰랐던 것이 아니라, 그의 어머니가 더 좋은 것을 하는 줄을 몰랐었다. 주인이 아니면서 주인처럼 거만하고 게으른 것이 추악하듯이, 종이 아니면서 종처럼 비천하고 부지런한 것은 아름다웠다. 세상에 주인이 어디 있고, 종이 어디 있는가. 주인 행세하는 사람치고 종 아닌 사람 없고, 종 처신하는 사람치고 주인 아닌 사람이 없었다. 그때 그는 어려서 그런 것을 다 몰랐을 것이다. 다만, 잘난 남자와 못생긴 여자가 부부라는 것이 충격이었고, 못난 여자가 잘난 남자보다 더 훌륭할 수 있다는 것이 또 충격이었다. 보통 때 같았으면 그는 그런

fighting until their lives are in danger. No one can accuse them of wanting to go to war. When lives are at stake, even beasts spit poison. Take the snake, for instance. Doesn't bite if you don't step on it. Snakes are wary if you wave a stick at them, so imagine how frightened they'll be if a person walked by. It would be like seeing a mountain move. Even so, they don't bite. If you don't bother them, they steal a few glances at you, stick their tongues out and curse at you, and then go their way. They probably don't swear either. They're allowed to grumble to themselves. Did the war begin because the puppet army invaded?[9] Which puppets? Whether it's the puppet army from the north verses the national army, or the People's Army verses the ROK Army, they fight because they're the same. The same? How can the People's Army and the ROK Army be the same? How can defending freedom and brutal communizing be the same? Aren't they complete opposites? If soldiers aren't the same as soldiers, who would you compare them to? All soldiers are the same. All wars are the same wars. No point in distinguishing between friend and foe. Evacuation means going to a place without armies, without guns, where guns aren't

것들을 무심히 보아 넘겼을 것이다. 마지막일지도 모른
다는 생각까지는 아니더라도, 그 비슷한 마음이 그의
눈을 비범하게 만들었을 것이다. 피난이 어디 예삿일인
가. 평생에 한 번도 너무 많았다.

그들은 작은 산을 넘었다. 바다가 나왔다. 물의 끝에
있는 포구의 이름은 화포였다. 고깃배들이 몇 척 한가
롭게 떠 있었다. 물가는 모래밭이 아니라 자갈밭이었
다. 비록 몇 십 리였지만 강행군 몇 시간에 다다른 바닷
가는 위안이었다. 설마 바다 위를 걸어갈 수는 없었다.
터벅터벅 걷기의 끝이었다. 현실적 계산이 아니더라도
바다는 시원했다. 끝간 데를 모르겠는데, 막힌 데가 없
었다. 저만치 섬들이 몇 덩이 떠 있었지만, 그것들은 바
다가 툭 트인 것을 더 돋보이게 할 뿐이었다. 저쪽은 어
디일까. 갈 수 없는 곳이었다. 배를 타면 갈 수 있었지
만, 그들의 눈앞에 떠 있는 작은 돛배로 갈 수 있는 곳은
바다의 저쪽이 아니라 중간이었다. 뭍과는 달리 물은
아무리 멀리 떨어졌어도 저쪽과 이쪽이 서로 닿았다는
느낌이 들었다. 멀고도 가까웠다. 멀면 잊고, 가까우면
갔다. 멀어서 갈 수 없고, 가까워서 잊을 수 없었다. 갈
수도 없고 잊을 수도 없고, 가슴만 설레었다. 그는 검푸

fired, and if fired, rarely do harm. Why Palgeumsan of all places? Why not Palgongsan—"gong" for "empty"—rather than the temporary capital? There's got to be an unoccupied mountain where the moon shines brightly by night somewhere in Joseon. The armies move like clouds, the gunshots fill the air, and shooting leads to plundering. What choice have we got? Let's go somewhere where shooting doesn't lead to injuries and injuries don't hurt as much. And where would that be? The countryside. Why the countryside? There's more nature in the countryside than there are people. It's the opposite in the cities. More people than nature. What are guns? Human inventions. Man's creation had influence among men, but was powerless before Heaven's creations.

They fled to the south. Southwest to be precise. The army from the North had not invaded yet, and the army fleeing to the Southeast was long gone. In military terms, these were unoccupied communities, unoccupied *terrain*. Nothing was different. One was better off without things that had little influence, that would not be missed when they were gone. These things were like tumors—unnecessary and harmful if unlucky. They buried their crockery

른 자갈밭에 주저앉아 넋을 놓고 바다의 끝을 바라보았다. 돌들은 계란만했다. 큰 것은 거위알만한 것도 있었다. 물결이 기어올라와 부서지면 흰 거품들을 남기고 돌들 사이로 잦아들었다. 명사십리처럼 검은 깻돌들이 한 이삼백 보 바다를 포근하게 안고 있었다. 기울기는 하얀 모래밭보다 조금 더 급했다. 검은 돌이 하얀 모래가 되자면, 물결들이 몇 번이나 부딪혀서 산산조각이 날까. 물에 씻기고, 소금에 절이고, 바람에 바래고, 햇볕에 그을리기 천 년 만 년, 사람의 뼈는 그동안이면 가루가 되고 먼지가 되어 흔적도 없이 사라질까. 돌멩이만도 못한 뼈, 그것도 썩은 뼈, 그것을 산꼭대기에 묻으면 어떻고, 갈아서 가루를 바람에 뿌리면 어떻고, 바다에 던지면 어떠냐. 금시발복이면 몇 대를 가고, 몇 대면 몇 년이냐. 돌멩이만도 못한 걸 가지고 웬 수선은 또 그렇게 요란하냐. 어른들은 때로는 어린이들보다 더 철이 없었다. 아마 전쟁도 철없는 어른들의 불장난이었다. 그는 돌멩이를 만졌다. 자세히 보니 검은 바탕에 흰 점들이 수없이 나 있었다. 가만있자, 사람은 살고 돌은 죽었다. 혹시 돌멩이도 살아 있는 것이 아닐까? 다만, 몸놀림이, 가령 거북이처럼 더딘 것뿐이었다. 엄청나게

in the ground, divided their food in bags and bundles, and set out on the journey. After twenty *li*, they came upon their ancestral burial ground. The burial ground was as peaceful as it had been all the other times they had passed by the cemetery. There were no refugees there, let alone soldiers. Nothing was different. If anything was different, they were.

Their anticipation of soldiers or refugees showing up turned the peaceful stillness of their journey into a chilling silence. Fleeing made their home a place to flee from. Near the cemetery, they got off of the main road in favor of the footpaths along the rice paddies and traveled another ten *li*. They passed villages with names that sounded familiar. The boy had never been to these villages before, but some students in his class were from these places. The awe that comes from discovering the great disparity between the name and the thing it refers to momentarily distracted the boy from his blistered, weary feet. The real thing was always different from the image its name conjured.

The real thing was larger and more complex than the name suggested. It was generally dirtier and shabbier, but there were so many things unlike

더 더딘 것뿐이었다. 뼈다귀가 살 속에 묻혀서 백 년 가고, 차돌이 풍우에 시달리면서 만 년을 간다면, 그 돌이 눈 한 번 껌뻑이는 데 한 시간이 걸리고 하루가 걸린다고 놀랄 일이 아니었다. 눈 한 번 감고 뜨는 데 한 시간이 흘러가고 하루해가 저문다면. 사람들이 그것을 옆에서 알아채지 못하는 것도 무리는 아니었다. 시계의 시간바늘 가는 것이 보이냐? 그는 돌멩이들을 물끄러미 들여다보았다. 아니, 이것이 어찌된 일이냐? 작은 흰 점들이 움직이는 것 같았다. 분명히 그것들이 스물스물 꿈틀거리기 시작했다. 눈을 뜨는지, 입맛을 다시는지, 콧구멍을 벌름거리는지는 알 수 없었다. 아니, 그것이 아니었다. 돌은 사람처럼 방정맞지 않았다. 돌은 느리게 움직였고, 더딘 동작은 육안으로 볼 수 없었다. 아마 스물거린 것은 그의 눈이었다. 그는 눈이 침침해졌다. 그는 눈을 깜짝거렸다.

"뭘 허냐? 안 들리냐?"

그는 깜짝 놀랐다. 형이 그의 등 뒤에 와 있었다. 그는 나쁜 짓 하다가 들킨 것처럼 얼굴을 붉혔다.

"왜? 무슨 소리? 파도소리? 잘 들려."

"엄니가 니 부른다."

their names that the boy hardly noticed. But the boy's sense of awe was short-lived; his legs hurt again, his back ached, and his shoulders felt sore. Ten *li* on the footpath was longer than twenty *li* on the main road. Owing to the scenery, their journey felt increasingly less like a flight the farther they traveled. They were the only refugees. They gradually forgot that they were fleeing. Were they fleeing from or to the place they were now passing through? If it was the latter, how was it different from the place they had left behind, and if it was the former, how much longer before they were free from turmoil? Had they already crossed the line between life and death? No? No. Was the line following them? Was the line closing in? Where was the line between life and death? The spot where two armies battled each other? The front where one army chased its fleeing foe? If the line reached the shore, did they have to jump into the sea? If not, would they be engulfed by that line and become part of that army? Were they fleeing into the heart of war? This much was clear: fleeing was abandoning one's hometown. Fleeing was going from a place where people were fleeing to a place where people were not. A place of refuge was

"왜?"

"왜, 왜, 하지 마라. 니는 밥 안 묵냐? 저녁밥 묵을라면 물 길러 오니라."

"성은?"

"나는 나무하러 산에 간다. 쌀만 있으면 밥이 되냐?"

"물독에 물은?"

"니냐? 니가 그 물 썼냐? 그 물 때문에 난리가 났다."

"먹을 감았더니 온몸이 톡톡 쏘길래 한 바가지 뒤집 어썼어."

"니는 니 생각만 허냐? 갯가에서 물이 얼마나 귀한지 모르냐?"

"여름에 바닷가에 와서 해수욕헌 것이 잘못이야? 바닷 물에 들어갔다 나와서 민물에 몸 헹군 것이 잘못됐어?"

"아침에 길러다논 물이 바닥이 났다고 주인 여자가 방 안에서 투덜대는 바람에 엄니가 얼마나 속상한 줄 아냐?"

"떠다노면 될 것 아니야?"

"부엌 바닥에 물은 또 왜 그렇게 찌끄러놨냐? 한강이 라고 난리더라."

"그게 정제야, 토방이지? 토방도 아니고 바로 마당이

where people were settled, wherever that may be.

The boy thought that the flight could take them anywhere. The closer the better. Dragging his tired legs along seemed to serve little purpose apart from getting him far away from his home. But his father thought differently. In the event of a crisis, it was wise to get as far from home as possible. Avoiding turmoil was avoiding familiar faces. They stopped for lunch at an acquaintance's house in the valley under a jagged mountain. Even there they had people they knew.

Ppolloksan was a rock mountain on a flatland. It was not very tall, but it was a conspicuous tower from a distance. The boy had never been to the base of the mountain until then, but had gazed at it many times from the family grave ten *li* away. According to the chief of the village, that mountain was a guardian mountain. The summit of the mountain was famous as an auspicious spot.

"During hard droughts, we pray for rain up there. We bring shovels and pickaxes."

"Why do you bring tools?"

"People secretly bury their ancestors up there at night. But burying the dead there brings drought. One man's blessing means famine for the rest."

더라. 마당이 바로 동네 길이더라."

"정제가 따로 있냐, 밥해 묵으면 정제지? 하여튼 니는 가는 데마다 말썽 안 부리면 어디가 근질근질허냐? 물 어끈 것도 니였구나?"

"몸 씨근디 물 안 어끄냐? 성이 물 떠와."

"니가 나무헐래?"

"그래, 물 뜨러 가면 꼭 벌 받는 것 같어. 나무허는 것 이 더 쉽기도 하고."

"산에 가는디?"

"방법이 있어. 엄니 화 많이 났냐? 니는 왜 가는 디마 다 일이 꼬이는지 몰라. 삼살방이 끼었냐?"

"니가 꼬일 일이 뭣이 있냐?"

"바닷물 속에 사람 살갗을 쏘는 독충이 있어."

"독충에 물렸으면 니가 시방 여기 이러고 있겄냐?"

"독초든지."

"미생물이었겠지. 지금은 괜찮냐?"

"아무렇지도 않아. 맑은 물속에 아무리 모래밭 조깨 없다고 자갈밭은 밭 아닌가 왜 독미생물이 있고, 그 흔 하고 흔한 물이 귀할 것은 무엇이고, 귀한 물이라도 그 렇지 떠다노면 될 것을 언제 봤다고 물 한 바가지 가지

214

"If the water gathers in one place, it will cause a great flood. Do you think outsiders bring bodies here?"

"People in the know come from neighboring villages bearing bones wrapped in cotton cloth and make flat graves."

"People come from far away, too. Long ago, Nurhaci's mother's virginity was taken by a monster living in a lake. She bore a son who grew up to love playing by the water, which worried the woman. She groaned: Like father, like son. A sage passing by one day saw a pit in the lake and admired it greatly. He produced a box for Nurhaci who happened to be playing in the water. He said that Nurhaci would be rewarded if he put the box deep into the pit for him. So Nurhaci..."

"Don't interrupt. The adults are speaking."

"It's okay. Children shouldn't be interrupted either. Tut tut."

"You're rambling. Make it short."

"Yes, sir. So Nurhaci..."

"It's already too long. Stop."

"Give it up. I'm taking over," said the boy's brother.

"It's okay. It's a good story."

고 동네 소드레를 꾸미고, 엎질러진 물이야 오뉴월 땡볕에 돌아서면 마를 것을 무슨 한강이고 섬진강이고."

"살이 낀 것이 아니라 부모 속 썩인 벌인갑다."

"누가 언제? 먼 바다 바라보고 앉아 있는 것도 속 썩이는 거냐? 먹 감은 것 말고."

"꼭 재앙을 떨어야 속상하냐? 부모가 어려울 때 옆에서 조심 안 허는 것은 속 안 상하냐?"

"뭐 어려운 일 생겼어? 집 떠나면 다 고생이지."

"배 교섭이 잘 안 되는갑다. 원래는 여기서 안 자고 오늘 배를 타고 여기를 떠나게 돼 있다."

"돈?"

"결국 돈이지 뭐. 턱없이 선가를 높이 부른갑다. 펑계는 난리지만, 뭐, 난리가 시방 여기까지 왔냐? 바다에 인민군이 떴냐? 어뢰가 바다를 청소라도 하냐?"

"큰일났다. 걸어갈 수도 없고."

"배가 안 되면 백 리 길을 걸어야지. 차야 더 없다. 다 징발되고."

"섬 아니야? 물 위를 걷냐?"

"육지다. 큰길로 나가서 큰길로 큰길로 칠팔십 리 걸어가면 나온다."

"So the young Nurhaci pretended to put the box in the emperor meridian as promised, but he secretly put it in the wealth meridian. Then he went home and asked where his father was buried, exhumed his bones from the lake, reburied them in the emperor meridian, and Nurhaci went on to revive his country and become emperor."

"So rude."

"What? It was short."

They spread out a straw mat in the yard and gathered at a round table for lunch. They had wild vegetables, pickled greens, steamed eggs, bean paste soup, and white rice. They were used to the menu, but the food, made by someone else's hands, tasted unfamiliar. Food that did not take much to make could taste very different depending on who made it. First of all, there was a great amount of food. A big mound of rice spilled over the porcelain rice bowls placed before the young boys. It seemed like they had been given two bowls' worth. This was the portion of a grown man. The boys were pleased because they were hungry, but also because they were being treated like grownups. They emptied their bowls faster than the adults. Their host in white pants looked

"바다로 가면 빠르냐? 안 돌고 직선으로 가냐?"

"쪼금. 차만 있으면 육로가 빠르지."

"그 쪼깜 보고 이 항구까지 왔냐? 나는 바다 건너 산 동반도나 상해라도 가는 줄 알았다."

"이 멍청아, 육지로 가면 광주서 동부전선으로 진격하는 인민군하고 조우한다. 한바탕 회전이라도 헐래?"

"전쟁을 피해 간 것이 아니라 만나로 갔냐?"

"엄니 말이 그 말이다. 엄니는 있자커니, 아부지는 가자커니."

"떠났는디 있잔 말이 왜 또 나오냐?"

"일이 잘되냐? 잘 풀릴 줄 알고 나온 건 아니지만, 이렇게 폭폭헐 줄은 몰랐지."

"떠나자는 말이 다 책임진다는 말은 아니다. 같이 고생하자는 말이다. 봇짐 싸기가 불행이지, 길 떠났으면 참아야지."

"참자니 화가 나지. 물이나 길러 와. 아니, 나무나 해 오니라."

"성이 나무해. 이 자갈밭에 자잘한 나무토막들 많아. 저 모퉁이 돌아가면 큰 것들도 있어. 몇 끄니는 문제없어."

"임자 없냐?"

like a scholar rather than a farmer. The woman in her colored dress looked like hired help from the village rather than the lady of the house.

The man had a finer appearance than the woman, both in looks and conduct. She was scrawny, had a small face, and eschewed attention. The hard work of the household had mainly fallen on her, but she did not like to show her face. The man ate with their father, but she did not eat at the women and children's table. She continued to wait on them throughout the meal and retreated to the kitchen for a hurried snack of leftovers when everyone else had finished. In other words, the man was the lay-about of the house, and she was the worker. It went without saying that she did all the chores, and while the man may have helped with the rice farm-ing, the vegetable farm was likely entirely her re-sponsibility. Aside from the two small children that clung to their mother's hem, there seemed to be no evidence of her authority in the house. She worked like a slave as their mother had, but was unlike their mother in that she did not assume the role of the matriarch. Their mother was both.

Until then, it had never occurred to the boy that his mother worked like a slave. Watching the

"물결이 임자야. 씻겨서 빽따구 같애."

"물가에서 나무허냐?"

"산에 가서 물 뜨기지."

그는 양동이들을 가지고 산으로 물을 길러 갔다. 그의 어머니가 하나만 가지고 가라는 것을 들은 척도 않고 양 손에 하나씩 둘을 들고 갔다. 주인 여자가 양철 물통 찌그러진다고 고시랑거렸다. 그가 화를 낸 것은 불발이었다. 터졌다면 잘못 터졌다. 누가 물통들 몇 개를 들고 나간다고 놀랄 사람 같으면 아예 물 한 쪽박에 수선을 피우지 않았다. 샘은 논이 끝나고 산이 시작되는 곳, 산자락 끝에 있었다. 물을 가득 채운 물통은 무거웠다. 하나도 그에게는 과했다. 그의 분노는 불발이거나 오발이 아니라 그에게서 터졌다. 그는 백 걸음도 안 되는 논두렁길을 물 두 통들을 들고 끙끙거리며 돌아왔다. 물은 참 귀했다. 그런 물로 몸을 씻느니 차라리 냄새나는 것이 좋았다. 그의 분통이 겨냥된 사람한테서 안 터지고 쏜 사람한테서 터진 것이 이상하지도 억울하지도 않았다. 물 한 초롱이 그냥 흘러가는 물이 아니라는 것을 알았더라면 그가 누구한테 분통을 터뜨리고 말고가 없었다. 그의 분노는 불발도, 오발도, 자폭도 아니었다. 말하

woman do chores around the house, he under-stood how his mother's work differed from hers. Working like a slave did not seem bad. It didn't matter if she was working like a slave or a master; work never seemed so noble and beautiful as it did then. Work was to be done like you were a slave, not like you were a master. The boy's mother han-dled supervision, extravagance, pride, and lethargy like a master. The master and the slave each had their own role to play. If one played both master and slave, the brilliance of hard labor would be obscured in the shadow of laziness. Hard work was hard, easy work was easy. Handling both kinds of work was no small task, and doing hard work well was more admirable than trying to do both. The next best thing to do was to handle both roles well. Playing only the master's role well was worse than being unable to handle either. In other words, this was the worst option. His mother swung back and forth between the first and second options. She was usually on the second option.

Before, the boy had not known that the first op-tion existed. He believed that the second option was the first option. He thought that what his mother did was the best option. When it became

자면 공포였다. 지나놓고 보니 처음부터 빈 깡이었다. 분통의 결과가 분통의 원인을 없애버렸다. 그만 괜히 혼자 붉으락푸르락, 차치고 포치고, 장고치고 북쳤다. 주인 여자가 부화뇌동하지 않고 태연자약한 것이 고맙기까지 했다.

그들이 화포를 떠난 것은 이튿날 점심 뒤였다. 맑은 바닷물에 쐐기가 있는 것도 별났지만, 밤에 포구에 모기가 없었다. 갯가 깔다구가 돛배를 뚫었다. 그 극성맞은 각다귀가 다 어디로 갔냐. 포구 이름이 불 화자 화포일시 분명했다. 불기운 때문에 바닷물이 따끔거리고, 유충이 풍요로운 바닷가에서 성충으로 번창하지 못했다. 밤에 밤기운과 만난 불기운이 바닷물 위로 푸르스름한 요기를 깔았고, 그 너울거리는 도깨비불들이 길 잃은 날파리들을 쫓았다. 그곳은 하룻밤 하룻낮을 머물렀지만, 여러 날을 보냈던 딴 고장보다 더 그의 마음을 사로잡았다. 그들이 거기서 배를 타고 가는 곳의 이름을 들었을 때 그곳은 한층 더 그의 마음속에서 신비스러워졌다. 그들이 화포를 떠나서 가는 곳은 대포였다. 대포라니, 이 귀빠진 벽지에 대포라니, 도대체 얼마나 큰 항구이길래 그런 대포를 트냐? 화포가 화포인 것을

clear to him that there was something better, his belief that his mother had been performing the duties of the first option from the start, always had, and always would, did not turn out to be completely wrong. It was not that he hadn't known that there was something better than what his mother did, but he had not known that his mother handled herself with a grace and tact beyond the boy's comprehension.

As unseemly as it was for someone who was not a master to behave as arrogantly and lazily as a master, it was beautiful for someone who was not a slave to act as humbly and diligently as a slave. There were no masters or slaves in the world. Everyone who behaved like masters were, in fact, slaves, and everyone who behaved like slaves were the true masters. The boy was too young then to understand this. However, he was shocked that a handsome man and a homely woman could be a couple, and shocked once again that a homely woman could be more esteemable than a handsome man. Under different circumstances, he would have overlooked something like this. Something resembling an impending end must have anointed him with the insight. Fleeing from war

보니, 가봐야 알겠지만, 대포도 틀림없이 또 하나의 돌 틈이나 뒷개나 물치나 물안빠지였다.

그들이 타고 간 배는 작은 고기잡이 나무 돛배였다. 말로만 듣던 여객선이나 군함에다 대면 작았다. 그가 본 배들 중에서는 어쩌면 가장 컸다. 집채만 했다. 집이 한 채 동네 앞 물 위에 둥둥 떠 있었다. 지붕은 물론 없었다. 배는 그들을 다 태우고 짐까지 다 싣고 나서도 아직 덜 찼다. 고물에 베잠방이를 허리에 홀쳐입고 구릿빛으로 그슬린 웃통에 베적삼을 걸친 한 주름 많은 중늙은이가 가늘고 긴 막대기를 들고 서 있었다. 배가 발밑에서 움직였지만, 그는 마치 그의 집 앞마당에서 남들 출어하는 것을 구경이라도 하는 것처럼 쉽고 탄탄하게 서 있었다. 그는 배가 솟으면 그도 솟고, 배가 잦으면 그도 잦았다. 배가 왼쪽으로 기울면 그도 왼쪽으로 기울었고, 오른쪽으로 쏠리면 그도 오른쪽으로 쏠렸다. 그는 배의 자연스러운 한 부분이었다.

그의 몸은 배의 널빤지가 전해오는 충격들을 부드럽게 빨아들였다. 그의 몸이 부드러웠다. 그들은 반대였다. 그들의 몸은 바로 그 널빤지처럼 단단하고 뻣뻣해서 배의 요동을 하나도 받아들이지 못하고 모조리 되튀

was a big deal—once in a lifetime was once too many.

They climbed a small hill. They reached the ocean. The name of the small port on the edge of the water was Hwapo. A few fishing boats floated idly on the water. On the edge of the water was a pebble beach rather than a sandy one. They had only traveled a few dozen *li* but seeing the ocean after following a tight schedule was a great comfort to them. No one could suggest they continue on and walk across the sea. Their grueling march had come to an end. Despite their circumstances, the sea was refreshing. It stretched on and on without an end in sight. A few clusters of islands floated far out in the ocean, but they only served to accentuate its immensity. What lay beyond it? It was an unreachable place. A ship could take them there, but the small sailboat that bobbed on the water before them seemed it could only take them halfway there and no further. Unlike the land, the water seemed to connect this shore with that shore no matter how immeasurable the expanse. It was far, yet near. When far, it was forgotten. When near, one could travel to it. It was too far to travel to, and too near to forget. Unreachable and unfor-

졌다. 그들의 몸뚱이들은 배가 출렁이는 대로 나무토막들처럼 나뒹굴려고 했다. 그들은 뱃전 위에 나가떨어지지 않으려고 무진 애를 썼다. 허벅지와 장딴지에 쥐가날 정도였다. 물렁물렁한 사람은 단단한 배의 일부였고, 단단한 사람들은 단단한 배와 끊임없이 싸웠다.

노인이 물속에 꽂힌 삿대에 힘을 주자 배가 미끄러지기 시작했다. 배가 원래 두둥실 움직이고 있었고 그들은 몸 가누는 데에 정신이 없어서 그들은 배가 떠나는 것을 알아차리지 못했다. 사공이 상앗대를 거둬들이고 배 옆쪽에 길게 뉘여 놓았던 길고 실팍한 노를 끌어내어 배의 뒷전 쇠붙이에 아귀를 맞추고 한 손으로 손잡이를 흔들흔들 젓자 물속에 잠긴 넓적한 노 끝이 물을 헤집고 배를 앞으로 밀었다. 배가 얼마쯤 나아간 뒤에사 사람들은 배가 출항한 줄을 알았다. 영감이 농담처럼 노를 몇 번 쥐어박자 금방 눈앞에 있던 동네가 저만치 멀어져갔다. 그것으로 사람들은 배가 가는 것을 짐작했다. 참, 자전거는 앉아서 달음박질하기라더니, 배타기는 제자리에 서서 달리기였다. 말하자면 축지법이었다. 빨리 가려면 발을 부지런히 놀려야겠지만, 땅을 줄이는 것도 방법이었다. 땅은 금세 멀어졌다. 사공은 두

gettable, it made waves in the heart.

The boy sprawled out on the dark blue pebble beach and gazed at the sea horizon as though his spirit had escaped from him. The pebbles were as big as eggs. Some large ones were as large as goose eggs. Waves crawling up the pebbles fell to pieces and melted into the rocks, leaving behind a white foam. The black pebbles like the ones in Myeongsasimni up in Hamgyeong-do embraced two to three hundred paces of the ocean in its welcoming arms. The pebble beach was steeper than white, sandy beaches. How many times did the waves have to shatter against the black rocks until the rocks turned to white sand? Washed by the water, pickled in the salt, faded in the wind, and roasted under the sun for thousands, tens of thousands of years while the bones of man turn to powder, then to dust, then nothing. Bones, rotten bones at that, were nothing compared to rocks. So what did it matter if they were buried on top of the mountains, or scattered in the winds, or dissolved in the ocean? How many generations had been blessed by good fortune, and how many more years of good fortune would an auspicious gravesite amount to? Why all the fuss over a lifes-

손들로 힘들여 노를 저었다. 노는 배를 밀기도 하고 또 배의 방향을 틀기도 했다. 똑같이 노를 흔드는 것 같았지만, 노 끝이 물살을 가르는 각도가 조금 달랐고, 그 차이가 배의 진로를 잡았다. 배가 연안을 벗어나 공해상에 이르자, 늙은 사공이 노를 거둬들이고 배 한복판에 세워진 돛대에 돛을 올렸다. 돛은 누더기였다. 말아서 배 한쪽에 보드락쳐 놓았을 때는 저것이 무엇인고 했고, 무엇인지 알았을 때는 그것이 무슨 힘을 쓸꼬 싶었는데, 태극기 올리듯이 줄을 잡아당겨 그것이 푸른 하늘에 활짝 기지개를 펴자 그런 위용이 또 없었다. 순풍에 돛단배였다. 망망대해, 이제는 제법 무엇이 쏜살같이 미끄러져 간다는 느낌이 들었다. 아마 시원하게 부는 바람 때문이었다. 바람이 불어서 배가 가는데, 배가 가니 또 바람이 불었다. 사공 영감은 한 손에 돛줄을 잡고, 또 한 손에 키 손잡이를 붙잡았다. 여름바람 정할소냐, 바람이 부는 대로 그는 줄을 놓았다, 잡았다, 댕겼다 했고, 키는 이따금씩 생각이 나면 심심풀이로, 또는 그것이 아직 그의 손아귀 속에 얌전히 들어 있는지 알아보려고 건드렸다. 그는 그 배의 선장이자 조타수이자 기관장이었다. 그리고 배의 구석구석을 잘 알고 아끼는

pan that was nothing compared to the life of a pebble? Adults were sometimes more foolish than children. The war was perhaps also the doing of foolish adults playing with fire.

He held a pebble in his hand. He looked closely and saw a million little specks on it. Wait a minute. Man was alive, and the pebble was dead. Perhaps pebbles were once living things? Only, they were as slow as turtles. If bones lasted a hundred years while buried in the flesh and pebbles lasted ten thousand years as they endured the wind and the rain, then perhaps it was no surprise if it took a pebble an hour or a day to blink. If a pebble spent an hour or a day just closing and opening its eyes, it was no surprise that no one noticed it. It would be as inconspicuous as the movement of the hour hand. The boy examined the pebbles. The tiny white dots seemed to be moving. They really did begin to wobble around. They were perhaps blinking, smacking their lips, or flaring their nostrils. No, no. Pebbles were more solemn than people. The rocks moved slowly, and the human eye could not detect their slow movement. It was probably his eyes that wobbled. His vision blurred. He blinked.

것으로 보아 아마 선주였다. 돛을 올린 지 한 시간쯤 되었을 때 배는 공해를 벗어나 다시 영해로 들어갔다. 멀리 푸르스름하게 떠 있던 땅끝의 산들이 눈앞으로 다가왔다. 그들은 그동안 쭉 잠시도 땅을 시야에서 놓친 적이 없었다. 배는 거의 육지로 둘러싸인 거대한 호수를 항해했다. 그들은 그동안 내내 순천만 안에 있었다.

배가 물에 닿았다. 삿대로 배를 모래밭에 접안한 선장이 높은 뱃전에서 물속으로 툭 뛰어내려 배를 땅 위로 끌어올리고 밧줄로 이물을 육지에 묶었다. 부두에는 아무것도 없었다. 집도 사람도 선창도 방파제도. 그것이 대포 포구였다. 사람들이 징검다리 건너듯이 널빤지 다리 위로 줄타기를 하고 배에서 내렸다. 짐을 다 풀자, 사공이 밧줄을 거둬 들고 배를 힘껏 민 다음 그 위에 올라탔다. 그가 삿대질을 하자 배가 뒤로 미끄러지기 시작했다. 담배 한 대 참은 쉬었다 감직도 하련만, 물땐지 바람땐지를 행여 놓칠세라 발이 땅에 닿기가 무섭게 다시 물속으로 뛰어드는 뱃사공의 날랜 몸놀림을 그는 모래 땅에 주저앉아 멍하게 바라보았다. 누가 냄비 뚜껑인지 양은솥 뚜껑인지를 찾는 것 같았지만 그는 벌로 들었다. 배가 떠났으니, 소두방 뚜껑이야 거기 있기 아니면

"What are you doing? Are you deaf?"

He jumped. His older brother had snuck up behind him. His face flushed as though he had been caught doing something.

"What? Why? Hear what? The waves? I hear them fine.

"Mother's calling you."

"Why?"

"Stop asking why, why. Aren't you going to eat? If you're going to eat, go fetch some water."

"What about you?"

"I'm gathering wood. You can't make rice with just water."

"What about the water in the water jar?"

"It was you, wasn't it? You used that water! There was a big fuss about it because of you."

"My body was stinging after I went for a swim, so I poured a ladleful over myself."

"Always thinking of yourself. Don't you know that water's scarce on the beach?"

"What's wrong with going for a swim at the beach in the middle of summer? What's wrong with rinsing off with freshwater after going in the ocean?"

"The landlady came into the room and nagged mother's ear off about the water running out when

없기였다. 소란 피운다고 무슨 소용이냐. 있으면 찾을
필요가 없었고, 없으면 찾으나마나였다.

"아이, 니 아까 내가 꼭 붙들고 있으라고 준 냄비 보따
리 어쨌냐?"

"예, 예? 나, 나요? 나 말이요?"

"여그 니 말고 누가 또 있냐?"

"예? 나 말고요?"

"말끝 또빡또빡 받지 말고 보따리 내놔. 꼭 보듬고 있
으라는 것 어쨌냐?"

"보따리요? 아까 맨 먼저 땅에 내려놨는디."

보따리 위에 딴 짐들이 쌓여 있었다. 사공은 삿대를
거둬들이고 노를 저었다. 배가 방향을 돌렸다. 빈 배는
돛을 올리기도 전에 나는 듯이 미끄러져 갔다. 그것은
빠르게 작아졌다. 그는 그것을 바라보았다. 그것은 아
름다웠다. 그들이 표류해 온 난파선원들처럼, 동서남북
을 모르고 낯선 땅에 앉아서 쉬고 있을 때, 동네에서 전
갈을 받고 사람이 나왔다. 팔촌은 다들 논일 나가고 사
람이 없어서 혼자 왔다. 우선 사람들만 그를 따라 집으
로 가고, 짐은 나중에 들일 끝내고 일손이 들어오는 대
로 와서 지고 가는 것이 좋았다. 그들이 거처할 집은 외

she fetched it only just this morning. Mother's very upset."

"So what? I'll go fetch some more."

"And why did you have to make such a mess in the kitchen? The lady said you turned her kitchen into the Han River."

"That's not a kitchen. It's a mud hut! No, it wasn't even a hut. The kitchen was more or less in the yard and the yard was in the street!"

"The kitchen isn't some special place. Wherever you make food is the kitchen. Can't help making trouble wherever you go, can you? It was you who spilled water everywhere, wasn't it?"

"How do you wash yourself without spilling water? You fetch the water."

"And you'll gather wood?"

"Yeah, fetching water now feels like a punishment. Besides, gathering wood is easier."

"Even if you have to go into the mountain to get it?"

"I have a plan. Is Mother really angry? Nothing's been working out for me lately. Just my luck, I guess."

"What else is there to go wrong?"

"There are poisonous bugs in the water that sting

딴집이었다. 마침 염전 허는 손씨가 무인도에 손을 댔다가 송사가 붙어 게워내놓은 세 칸 와가를 그가 중간에 사람을 넣어서 우선 문중 것으로 잡아놓았다. 동네는 거기서 오 리쯤 떨어져 있었다. 짐을 들고 가자면 조금 멀었다. 그들의 생각은 달랐다. 그들은 손 아니냐? 아니, 그는 손 아니냐? 그가 지금 지고 가면 안 되냐? 그들이 짐을 하나씩 집어들었다. 짐을 두고 몸만 갈 수도 없거니와, 짐 옆에 무한정하고 앉아서 먼 바다 바라보기만 할 수도 없었다. 팔촌은 할 수 없다는 듯이 어디서 지게를 아무거나 하나 얼른 줏어왔다. 그는 그의 집도 그의 집, 남의 집도 그의 집이었다. 그의 집 지게도 그의 지게, 남의 집 지게도 그의 지게였다. 지게가 집에 있으나 들에 있으나, 임자가 옆에 있으나 멀리 있으나 마찬가지였다. 그의 것도 매한가지였다. 그가 안 쓰면 딴 사람들이 썼다. 쓰고 제자리에 두어도 되고, 쓴 자리에 두어도 되었다. 밥도 배고프면 급한 대로 아무 집에나 들어가서 소두방 뚜껑을 열었다. 있으면 먹고, 없으면 보탰다. 집에 흔한 돌담 하나 없고, 있어도 허리참을 안 넘고, 다 쓰러져가는 사립문은 항상 활짝 열렸거나 아예 없었다. 담이 없으니 내 집, 네 집이 없었다. 있어도 등

you."

"If they were poisonous, you wouldn't be standing here now."

"Or poisonous plants."

"Microorganisms. Are you okay now?"

"All better. A pebble beach is no different from a sandy beach, so what are these microorganisms doing in the clean water? Water isn't scarce. It's everywhere. Even if it is scarce, you can always fetch more. Who does she think she is, kicking up a fuss all over the village over one scoop of water? Besides, when you spill water on the ground it dries up in the blink of an eye in the summer sun, so don't go around calling wet ground the Han River or the Seomjin River."

"It's not bad luck. You're being punished for being a bad son."

"When have I ever been a bad son? Is staring off at the sea being a bad son? I'll admit I shouldn't have gone in the water, though."

"Being a bad son doesn't always mean making trouble. You have to watch yourself when things are tough for Father and Mother."

"Things aren't especially tough for anyone. This is normal for anyone who leaves home."

기소 토지대장이나 건물대장하고는 상구 달랐다. 들고 나고 먹고 멕힌 금을 바로잡자면 도시계획을 새로 해야 할 판이었다. 객지 사람이 등본을 떼어와서 측량을 한 번 했다가, 욕만 실컷 먹고 몰매를 겨우 면했다. 그것도 그가 나서서 말리는 바람에 그만했다. 그는 그의 친구 였다. 그가 끌어들인 것은 아니고, 그가 제 발로 찾아왔다. 외지 사람들이나 타성바지들이 고생이었다. 일가라 도 밖에서 들어오면 도로묵이냐? 무슨 소리. 일가는 어디 살아도 일가였다. 왜 도토리묵이냐? 타성씨들은 일년 아니라 십 년을 살아도 개꼬리였다. 타성들은 외지에서 오나 동네 안에서 오나 천덕꾸러기, 개밥에 도토리, 찬밥 신세냐? 일가는 오래 사나 처음 사나 한 식구냐? 그래. 그렇단 말이여. 어디 살면 핏줄에 물 섞이냐? 그는 성장헌 이래 객지를 많이 떠돌았다. 아무리 오래 나가 있다가도 돌아오면 언제나 고향이었다. 지금도 몇년 동안 바람 쐬고 돌아다니다가 돌아온 지 얼마 안 되었다. 돈 떨어지면 돌아오냐? 동네사람들이 좋아하냐? 고향 떠날 적에 빈손으로 나가는 것 아니고, 이것저것 돈 될 만한 것 손대고 없는 살림에 흔적 남기기 일쑤여서, 금의환향 아니면 출향관 빚을 잃고 야반도주 누명

236

"I think they're having a hard time finding a boat. We were supposed to leave by boat rather than staying the night here."

"Money?"

"It all comes down to money. Apparently they asked for an impossibly high fare. They're blaming the war, but the war isn't here yet. The North Korean army isn't waiting out in the sea. No torpedoes sweeping the sea."

"Darn. We can't very well walk there."

"If the boat doesn't work out, we'll have to go around the water a hundred *li* on foot. Cars are even harder to find than boats. They've all been requisitioned."

"Aren't we going to an island? Are we crossing the water on foot?"

"No, we're staying on the mainland. We can get there by making our way back to the main road and following it for about seventy to eighty *li*."

"Is it faster by sea? Is it a shortcut?"

"A little faster. Land is faster if there's a car."

"We came all the way to this port for 'a little faster?' I thought we were crossing the sea to get to the Shandong Peninsula or to Shanghai."

"Idiot. If we go by land, we'll run straight into the

쓰기 알맞았다. 살던 사람 나갔다가 돌아와도 그러한데, 듣도 보도 못헌 사람 처음 오면 어떠힐꼬. 그가 큰 짐 두어 개를 지게에 졌다. 지겟짐치고는 무거운 것도 아니었는데 팔촌은 지게질이 서툴렀다. 농촌에 산다고 반드시 지게를 잘 지라는 법은 없었다.

"팔촌은 지게가 등하고 따로 노요."

"가벼워서 그러네. 쌀 한 가마면 등더리에 찰싹 달라붙는다네."

"평소 지게를 가까이 안 허셨는갑소. 쌀 한 가마면 쌀가마가 사람을 지겄소."

"그러기도 허네. 내가 사무 볼 일이 좀 많은 편이라네."

"농어촌에 농사허고 어업 말고 또 무슨 사무가 있소?"

"그건 아우님이 모르는 소릴세. 공부 좀 헌 사람이면 농어촌에서 발 뺑고 편히 농어업에 종사하라고 가만 놔두지 않는다네. 관공서 공문도 시간 댈라면 급허지만, 군인 간 아들의 편지 답장이나 과부 연애편지도 당사자들헌테는 촌각을 다툰다네."

"기다리는 사람들헌테는 일각이 여삼추지요."

"그렇다네. 안 기다려본 사람은 그 속 모르지. 많은 것은 역시 관청 문서고, 관청 문서 중에는 송사 서류가 으

North Korean army. Want your own private battle?"

"Looks like we've come to greet the war, not run from it."

"That's what Mother's been saying. Mother says we should have stayed, Father says we were right to leave."

"We've already left. Why is she bringing that up again?"

"Things aren't going well. There was no guarantee that things would work out when we left, but we didn't know just how tough this would all be."

"Father said we should leave, he didn't say he'd be responsible for everything that happens along the way. He meant let's get through this together. Packing up and leaving is tragic, but we should be a little more patient now that we're on the road."

"Having to be patient is what's got Mother cross. So go fetch the water. Or rather, gather the wood."

"You gather wood. There're lots of branches and logs on the beach. I saw some big ones around the corner over there. That should do for a meal or two."

"They don't belong to anyone?"

"They belong to the waves. The waves washed them clean. Like bones."

뜸이네."

"담 없이 사는 동네에 송사가 웬 말이요?"

"밀고, 진정, 고소, 고발이 아마 동부육군에서 가장 많네. 말이 없다고 속조차 없을손가."

"객지에서 굴러온 사람들이 없으면 누구허고 싸우요?"

"동네에 타성바지 아니면 사람이 없을라고?"

팔촌은 땀을 흘렸다. 길이 너무 멀었다. 그의 생각이 옳았다. 그것은 짱짱한 오리였다. 그들의 대포살이가 시작되었다.

『베네치아에서 만난 사람』, 작가정신, 1999

"Gathering wood by the water?"

"Not unlike fetching water in the mountain."

The boy took the pails up into the mountain to fetch water. He ignored his mother who said he should just take one, and carried one in each hand. The landlady grumbled that he was denting her tin pails. The boy's anger was a dud, a defective fire-cracker. If it did explode, it exploded in vain. If the landlady had been the sort of woman who would be impressed by a boy carrying two pails of water, she would not have made a fuss over one ladleful of water. The well was at the end of the paddies at the foot of the hill. Once the pails were filled with water, they were heavy. One pail was too much for him. His anger was not a dud but a bomb he had dropped on himself. He scrambled the less than hundred paces back along the paddies with the two water pails. Water was scarce. He would rather stink than use precious water for washing. The boy did not find it strange or unfair that his anger exploded at himself rather than at the person his anger was aimed at. If he had known that a scoop of water was not just another scoop of water, he would not have been furious at anyone. His anger was not a dud, an accidental detonation, or a suicide bomb. It was fear. He learned after the fact that there was no substance to this anger. The result of the anger invalidated its cause. He had turned red in the face, huffed and puffed indignantly, and had a run around like a headless chicken for nothing. He was grateful the landlady remained completely unresponsive to anything he did.

The next day after lunch, they left Hwapo. It was strange to find stinging insects in the water, but stranger still to find no mosquitoes at night on a port. They say estuary mosquitoes can pierce through sails. What happened to those impetuous little creatures? The "hwa" of Hwapo must have meant "fire." The fire made the water sting and the mosquito larvae die before they could mature despite the plentiful nutrients the sea had to offer. At night, the fire clashed with the cold of the night and cast a blue, sinister aura over the water, and the billowing spirit fire shooed the flies. The boy's family stayed in Hwapo for only one day and one night, but the village captivated the boy more than the other villages where they had longer stays. The mystique of Hwapo grew in the boys' mind when he heard the name of the place they were to set sail for: Daepo.[10] Daepo? Out here in the middle of nowhere? How large was this port, and how big of a lie was its name? Considering what Hwapo turned out to be, they would not find out whether Daepo deserved its name until they saw the port for themselves, but it was sure to be another small crack in the rock, a mud flat, a drain, or a sea dike.

The boat they traveled on was a small wooden fishing sailboat. It was smaller compared to the ferries or carriers that the boys had only heard of, but it was perhaps the largest they had ever actually seen. It was as big as a house. A house was floating by the village shore. Of course, there was no roof. The boat carried the family and all of their luggage and still had room. At the stern, a wrinkled, aging man with the waist of his cotton pants drawn tight and his copper, sunburned chest visible under his cotton shirt stood with a long, thin pole. The boat shifted beneath their feet, but the boy stood as steady on his two feet as though he was standing in his front yard watching fishermen leave for sea. He rose and fell, and listed left and right with the boat. He was one with the boat.

His body gently absorbed any shock coming from the planks. His body was supple. But not the rest of his family. As hard and stiff as planks, they threw back all the movement of the boat. Their bodies seemed about to roll about the boat like logs as the boat rose and fell. They held on tight so as to not be thrown overboard. Their thighs and calves cramped. The supple became part of the rigid boat, and the rigid fought endlessly against it.

The old man pushed the pole through the water and the boat glided away from the shore. The boat was swaying to begin with, and they were so occupied with finding their balance that they did not notice the boat sailing away. The boatman drew up the punting pole and laid it down lengthwise along the side of the boat. He pulled out a pair of sturdy oars, mounted them on the oarlock near the stern, and shook them back and forth with one hand. Soon, the oar blades emerged from the water and pushed the boat forward. It was not until a while after the boat had set sail that its passengers realized they were on their way. The old man pushed the oars down a few times as though he was horsing around with the oars, and the village quickly receded from view. At this point, people knew that the boat was moving. If cycling was running while seated, sailing was running in place. In other words, it was the art of shrinking distance. In order to travel faster, moving your feet was certainly a good idea, but not as good as shortening the distance itself. Land drifted away quickly.

The boatman rowed hard with both hands. The oars pushed the boat and changed its direction. The movement seemed alike, but the subtle different in the way the end of the oar blade caught the current determined the course. When the boat pulled out of the coast and into open waters, the old boatman drew the oars in and raised the sail in the middle of the boat. The sail was in rags. When it had been folded and laid on the side of the boat, the boy had wondered what it was, and when he discovered its use, wondered what good it would do. But the sail, with its wings outstretched like a *Taegeukgi* against the clear blue sky, was as majestic as anything. They sailed in the gentle breeze.

In the vast, eternal ocean, the boat seemed to gain speed. It must have been the cool wind. The wind propelled the boat, and the propelled boat in turn created more wind. The boatman had the halyard in one hand and steered the helm with the other. The summer wind was not to be tamed; he released and pulled the rope in whichever direc-

245

tion the wind blew, and adjusted the helm only
once in a while just for the hell of it, to make sure
it was still sitting tight in his hands. He was the
captain, the helmsman, and chief engineer of this
boat. The way he knew his way around the boat
and cared for it, he was its owner as well. About an
hour after the sails were raised, the boat sailed
back to the coastal area. The mountains had been
floating in a greenish haze from far away but
turned vivid as they neared the shore. The land had
not once disappeared out of sight during their
journey. The boat had sailed across a large lake
mostly surrounded by land. They were in Suncheon Bay throughout the whole trip.

The boat docked. The captain pulled the boat up
to the beach with his pole, jumped into the water
from the high deck, dragged the ship up on the
beach, and secured the bow on land with a length
of rope. There was nothing in the port. No houses,
people, docks, or breakwater. This was Daepo
Port. The family disembarked by tottering down a
single plank lain between the deck and the beach.
Once their luggage had been unloaded, the boatman retrieved the rope, pushed the boat back out
on the water with all his might, and hopped on. He

pushed the boat away from the beach with the pole and glided seaward. He might have stayed for a cigarette break, but he had to hasten back before the current or the wind changed. The boy plopped down on the sandy beach and gaped at the old man as he nimbly jumped right back into the water. Someone was looking for a pot lid or a pan lid, but the boy was not paying attention. The boat left, so the lid was either here or there. Fussing over it would not change anything. If they had it, there was no need to look. If they did not have it, looking for it would not have made any difference.

"Hey, what did you do with the pot and pans bundle I gave you to keep safe?"

"Huh? What? Me? Are you asking me?"

"Who else is here besides you?"

"Besides me?"

"Stop repeating everything I say and give me the bundle. Where did you put the bundle I told you to hang onto?"

"The bundle? I put it on the ground first thing when I got off."

There were other bags piled on top of the bundle. The boatman drew the pole and rowed with the oars. The boat changed direction. The empty boat glided away before the sails were up, and quickly grew small. The boy watched the boat. It was beautiful. The family sat on the beach like sailors washed ashore after a shipwreck, not knowing east from west, catching their breath as they took in the strange world around them. A man who had received the family's telegram came from the village to fetch them. The cousin came alone as everyone else was working the fields. He suggested they leave their things here and come with him to the house. They would come back for their things later when the others returned from work. Their new home stood all by itself some distance outside the village. The house belonged to a Mr. Son from the salt mines who had gotten involved in procuring a deserted island and had ended up filing a lawsuit. He had to give up his three-bedroom tiled-roof house that the cousin had hired a middleman to obtain and register as clan property.

The village was about five *li* away from the house. It was a bit far to walk with luggage. But the family disagreed. The cousin could help. Couldn't he help them carry some of their things back? They each picked up a piece of luggage. They could not leave without their things. Otherwise they would have to endlessly stare off to the sea with their things piled next to them. The resigned cousin quickly fetched an A-frame carrier from somewhere. For him, his house was his house and someone else's house was also his house. His A-frame was his A-frame, and someone else's A-frame was also his. It did not matter if the A-frame was at home or in the field, or if the owner was nearby or far away. And vice versa. If he did not use it, someone else would. Sometimes they returned it where they found it and sometimes they just left it where they had finished using it. When someone was hungry, they could walked into any house and just open the pot lid. If there was food, they ate it. If there was none, they added food to it. The stone walls they were used to seeing around every house were nowhere to be found here. And if there were walls, they only came up to the waist. Straw gates lay in shambles and were always open. Or, there were no gates at all. Without walls, there was no line between what was yours and what was mine. Even if there was, it was always different from what was recorded in the land registry and building registry at the registry office. To re-establish the lines that had been pushed, pulled, taken, and given away, an entirely new city planning was necessary. Outside people once came with official papers from the registry, and barely escaped uninjured after the villagers reviled them. If the cousin had not stepped in at the right moment, violence would have ensued.

The cousin was a friend of the boy's father. The cousin did not bring him to the village, but the father had found his own way in. Outside people and non-clansmen suffered in the village. And clansmen who'd been away ? They didn't count, did they? Nonsense. Once a clansman, always a clansman, no matter where you lived. Why were non-clansmen treated poorly? Non-clansmen were always on the bottom rung whether they had lived one year or ten years in the village. And were non-clansmen still riffraffs, outcasts, and bottom-feeders, regardless of whether they arrived from the outside or if they were born here? Were clansmen still family whether they had lived here long or had just arrived? Yes. That's what I'm saying. Living somewhere else doesn't water down your blood.

Their father had wandered away from the village quite a bit in his adulthood, but no matter how long he had been gone, there was always a place for him at home. This time, too, he was returning after many years. Did people come back when they ran out of money? How did the rest of the clan feel about that? One never left home empty-handed. They took anything valuable and more often than not left a dent in the family savings. So if they weren't returning home with riches, they were crawling back with broken dreams of making it big in some faraway place. They were accused of stealing away in the middle of the night.

Not all clansmen are welcome here, so you can just imagine what it's like for a complete stranger who stumbles into our village. The cousin put the large bags on the A-frame. The load was not very heavy as far as A-frame cargo went, but the cousin fumbled with it. Not all countryfolk were handy with an A-frame.

"The A-frame's bouncing off your back, cousin."

"The bags are too light, is what it is. A *kama* of rice would keep it steady."[11]

"Been a long time since you used an A-frame? A *kama* of rice could carry you, cousin!"

"That's true. I often have clerical work to do."

"What's there to do besides farming and fishing in an agrarian/fishing village?"

"Things are changing, you see. If you've received a bit of education, they won't leave you to farming and fishing anymore. There's urgent reports to write for government offices, and even more pressing is writing letters to sons in the army or love notes for widows."

"Minutes go by like years for those who are waiting."

"Exactly. You don't know what it's like until you've waited for something. Most of the things I write are government documents—most of which are lawsuit papers."

"Lawsuits? In a village without walls?"

"We have the highest number of informers, petitions, charges, and accusations in the eastern six counties. We don't quarrel much, but that doesn't mean we don't harbor grudges."

"If there aren't any outside people who stick around, who do the villagers sue?"

"Clansmen or non-clansmen—people are people."

Sweat dripped from the cousin's face. It was a long way to the house. The cousin was right. The house was well over five *li* away. So began their life in Daepo.

252

1) Zhuge Liang. Chinese strategist from the Three Kingdoms Period; Liangshan Marsh: fictional location in *Water Margin*, a 14th century Chinese novel; Battle of Salsu: war between Goguryeo and Sui Dynasty in 612; The Imjin War: Japanese invasion of Joseon in 1592; Manchu Invasion: Manchu invasion of Joseon in 1636.

2) Battle of Red Cliffs. War during the Three Kingdoms Period in China.

3) *Yukchabaegi*. Korean folk song.

4) Tokbadki. Korean game similar to knucklebones. Often played with small pebbles.

5) The speaker is alluding to *Romance of the Three Kingdoms*.

6) The name *Bongsu* also means a signal fire.

7) *Noron* and *soron* are political factions from the Joseon Dynasty.

8) Terms of police and army units from Joseon Dynasty.

9) Puppet army. Both South and North Koreans use this pejorative term for the other army.

10) Homonym for "large port," "canon," and "lie."

11) *Kama*. A straw bag for transporting grains. One *kama* is roughly 80 kilograms.

Translated by Jamie Chang

해설

Afterword

보통 명사로 표현된 시대의 반어

이경재 (문학평론가)

「무자년의 가을 사흘」은 '무자년의 가을 사흘' '팔공산' '화포 대포'로 장이 나뉘어져 있으며, 한국 현대사의 비극인 14연대 반란 사건으로부터 한국전쟁까지를 다루고 있다. '무자년의 가을 사흘'이 1948년에 발생한 14연대 반란을 시간적 배경으로 삼고 있다면, '팔공산'과 '화포 대포'는 6·25를 배경으로 삼고 있다. "전쟁이 임박했다는 말은 그들에게 새삼스러워서 아무 감흥을 주지 못했다. 그들은 그동안 내내 전쟁 속에서 살았다"는 부분이 잘 보여주듯이, 「무자년의 가을 사흘」은 1948년 14연대 반란 사건에서 6·25로 이어지는 이데올로기적 대립과 그에 따른 일상화된 폭력의 풍경이 주요한 서사적

256

A Great Irony of the Times in Ordinary Terms

Lee Kyung-jae (literary critic)

Organized into a series of scenes—'Three Days of Autumn, 1948,' 'Palgongsan' and 'Hwapo and Daepo"—Su Jung-in's "Three Days of Autumn, 1948" covers the tragic period in contemporary Korean history, from the 14th Regiment Rebellion incident to the Korean War. While the temporal setting for 'Three Days of Autumn, 1948' is the 14th Regiment Rebellion that took place in 1948, that for 'Palgongsan' and 'Hwapo and Daepo' is the Korean War, which began in 1950. As shown well in the description, "News of impending war was no news or surprise to the villagers. They had lived in a state of war their entire lives," "Three Days of Autumn,

내용이다. 이 작품은 자전적인 요소를 적지 않게 지니고 있다. 서정인은 전남 순천에서 나고 자랐으며, 열세살이었던 1948년 무자년 가을에 반란군들이 사흘 동안 순천을 점령하는 일을 겪었다고 한다. 이때 서정인은 진압군에 의해 군용 짐차를 따라 북국민학교로 잡혀갔다가 어리다고 밤에 풀려난 경험이 있다. 또한 한국전쟁이 발발한 1950년에는 인민군이 석 달 동안 순천을 점령하였으며, 이때 서정인 일가는 소설에서처럼 순천에서 몇 십 리 떨어진 시골로 피난을 가기도 했다고 한다.

분단과 전쟁의 비극은 한국 현대 소설사에서 적지 않게 다루어진 주제이다. 서정인의 「무자년의 가을 사흘」이 여타의 작품과 구별되는 특징은 두 가지이다. 첫 번째는 핵심적인 초점화자로 어린아이를 등장시킨 것이고, 두 번째는 제목에서 드러나는 것처럼 역사적 사건의 고유명사를 모두 제거했다는 점이다.

어린이를 중심인물로 내세운 것은 무엇보다 전쟁의 폭력성과 비극을 드러내는 데 효과적으로 기능한다. "노장년이 잇속으로, 청년이 몸으로, 치르는 전쟁을 소년은 가슴으로 겪는다. 노장청년이 백 년 뒤 사람들이 잘 알 것을 안다면, 소년은 그들이 도저히 알 수 없는 것

1948" takes as its main narrative topic the ideological conflict connecting the 14th Regiment Rebellion of 1948 to the Korean War, and the resulting scenes of violence that had become routine. This work has more than a few autobiographical elements. Su Jung-in was born and raised in Suncheon, Jeollanam-do, and is said to have experienced as an eleven-year-old the occupation of Suncheon by the insurgent forces during the autumn of 1948. At the time, Su was captured by the repressive forces, taken to North Elementary School, then freed later that night on account of his young age. Also, when the Korean War broke out in 1950, North Korean forces occupied Suncheon for three months, during which time his family fled, as did the family in the story, to the countryside a few tens of *li* away from Suncheon.

The tragedy of the division and the war in the Korean peninsula is a theme often seen in contemporary Korean fiction. Yet two characteristics distinguish Su Jung-in's "Three Days of Autumn, 1948" from other works dealing with the theme. First, it takes a child as its crucial focalizer. Second, as its title exemplifies, it eliminates every proper noun and specific term associated with historical events.

을 안다"는 말처럼, 어린이야말로 전쟁의 쓰라림을 가장 절실하게, 그리고 정직하게 느낄 수 있는 존재이기 때문이다. 그래서 어리다는 사실은 전쟁을 이해하고 느끼는 데 장애가 아니라 장점이다. 또한 어린이의 순수한 시각을 통해서 "어른들은 때로는 어린이들보다 더 철이 없었다. 아마 전쟁도 철없는 어른들의 불장난이었다"와 같은 표현에서처럼, 전쟁을 일으킨 성인들에 대한 직접적인 비판이 가능해진다.

이 작품에서는 일반적으로 사용하는 '1948년 가을 사흘'이라는 말 대신 '무자년의 가을 사흘'이라는 말을 사용하고 있다. '무자년'이란 육십갑자에 바탕한 동양식 연도 표기 방법에 따른 명칭으로서, 60년에 한 번씩 돌아온다. 이러한 표기법은 자연스럽게 순환성과 영원성을 강조할 수밖에 없다. 이러한 용어를 제목으로 사용한 것에서 단적으로 드러나듯이, 「무자년의 가을 사흘」에서는 14연대 반란 사건과 한국전쟁이라는 역사적 대사건이 지닌 고유한 단독성보다는 여타의 전쟁과 공유하는 본질적인 비극성에 초점을 맞추고 있다. "총 든 군인들은 같았다. 모든 전쟁들은 같은 전쟁들이었다"는 명제 속에는 작가가 14연대 반란 사건과 한국전쟁을 바

Having a child as the central character works most effectively to expose the violence and the tragedy of war. For children are beings capable of feeling the trauma of the war the most intensely and honestly: "While the older man and the man in his prime waged wars for gain, and the young man fought with his body, the boy experienced wars with his heart. While men of all other ages were well aware of the actual facts and details people would remember a hundred years later, the boy experienced what they could never know. The boy knew war." Thus, youth is not an impediment but an advantage to understanding and feeling the war. Also, through the innocent vantage of a child, it is possible to criticize directly the adults who have started the war: "Adults were sometimes more foolish than children. The war was perhaps also the doing of foolish adults playing with fire."

The Korean title for this work literally translates to "Three Days of Autumn in the Year of Muja" instead of the more common "Three Days of Autumn in 1948." "The year of Muja" is another name for the year 1948, following the Eastern method of notating years based on the sexagenary cycle, meaning it comes around every 60 years. This type of nota-

라보는 작가의 기본적인 성격이 압축되어 있다. "북괴군하고 국군이 됐건, 인민군하고 국방군이 됐건, 같으니까 싸운다"는 표현 역시도 한국전쟁을 고유성보다는 일반성 속에서 사유하는 작가적 시각으로 인해 가능한 표현이다.

「무자년의 가을 사흘」은 중편 분량을 지니고 있는데, 서사적 육체의 대부분은 중편에 걸맞은 서사적 사건이 아니라 작가의 깊이 있는 사색에서 비롯된 여러 가지 에세이적 진술들이 차지하고 있다. 그러한 사색은 전쟁이나 인간 일반의 이치를 향하는 경우가 많다. 전쟁을 몸으로 아는 것과 머리로 아는 것의 차이에 대하여 이야기한다든가, 문화적 공백기가 발생하는 시대적 상황을 진단한다든가 하는 대목이 그러하다. 특히 "세상에 주인이 어디 있고, 종이 어디 있는가. 주인 행세하는 사람치고 종 아닌 사람 없고, 종 처신하는 사람 치고 주인 아닌 사람이 없었다"나 "소수 양반들이 잘 먹고 잘 살았던 왕조 때도 나라를 짊어진 것은 많은 상놈들이었지만, 나라가 망한 다음에도 명줄을 이은 것은 역시 그들이었다"는 문장 역시 오래 기억할만한 가치가 있는 사유의 기록이다.

tion inherently emphasizes cyclicality and perpetuity. The fact that this term is featured in the title clearly shows that the focus of "Three Days of Autumn, 1948" is not on the unique singularity of such grand historical events as the 14th Regiment Rebellion and the Korean War, but on the fundamental tragedy common to all wars. The proposition, "All soldiers are the same. All wars are the same wars," sums up the basic characteristic of the author's view on the 14th Regiment Rebellion and the Korean War. The statement, "Whether it's the puppet army from the North verses the national army, or the People's Army verses the ROK Army, they fight because they're the same," is also possible because of this authorial stance that considers the Korean War for its generality rather than its singularity.

While "Three Days of Autumn, 1948" is novella-like in length, most of its narrative body is comprised of numerous essayistic testimonies stemming from the author's profound contemplation, rather than narrative events more typical for a novella. Such contemplation tends to point to the general logic in wars and humans, as seen in the part of the story that discusses the differences between knowing a war with one's body and knowing

「무자년의 가을 사흘」에는 서정인 특유의 상대주의적 인식에 바탕한 언어 구사의 장기가 유감없이 발휘되고 있다. 상식을 뒤엎는 대화적 상상력을 바탕으로 유동적이고 부조리한 전쟁을 소설화한 것이다. 그것은 이 작품에서 인물 간의 대화에 나타나는 말꼬리 잇기와 뒤집기를 통해 성립하는 독특한 '반어체'에 잘 나타난다. "어린이 세계에 머물러 있는 어른도 볼품없지만, 어른 세계에 뛰어든 어린이도 볼썽사나웠다"나 "어린이들은 어른 행세를 해서 어린이를 없앴고, 어른들은 어린이 짓을 해서 어른을 없앴다"와 같은 대목에서 서정인의 문장 구사가 지닌 독특한 특징을 확인할 수 있다. '화포 대포'에서 이상주의자인 아버지는 이상주의인 공산주의를 피하고, 현실주의자인 어머니는 현실적 폭력인 전쟁을 무서워하지 않는 것 역시, "시대의 반어"를 표현한 것으로 이해할 수 있다.

it with one's head, and in the part that diagnoses the epochal circumstances leading to a period of cultural void. Other notable records of thought include: "There were no masters or slaves in the world. Everyone who behaved like masters were, in fact, slaves, and everyone who behaved like slaves were the true masters"; and "Under a monarchy where a small minority of noblemen are well fed and clothed, it is the vast majority of the lower class that bear the weight of the country, and it is the lower class who survive when the country falls."

Su Jung-in puts his distinct talent for linguistic command based on relativistic consciousness on full display in "Three Days of Autumn, 1948." His fictionalization of war in all of its turbulence and irrationality is rooted in a conversational imagination that defies common sense. This is well displayed in the work's unique "style of irony" generated by the conversations among its characters where they build on, and turn on, one another's utterances. The unique characteristic of Su Jung-in's skillful sentence construction can clearly be seen in passages such as "Adults being childish was unseemly, but children in the world of adults was ghastly" and

"Children acted like adults, thereby eliminating children. Adults acted like children, thereby eliminating adults." Finally, the idealistic father who evades the idealistic philosophy of communism and the realistic mother who is unperturbed by the real violence of war stand as further expressions of "the irony of the times."

비평의 목소리

Critical Acclaim

서정인은 우리의 의식을 지배하고 있는 관념들의 실제와의 괴리를, 실제의 왜곡을 폭로한다. 서정인의 소설이 재치 있는 말놀이의 재미를 듬뿍 안기면서도 섬세한 독서를 요구하는 것은 이 때문이다. 이 같은 상대주의와 이를 뒷받침하는 반성적 성찰은 독특한 문체를 낳으니, 대화체와 같은 말에 다른 의미를 부여하는 말꼬리 잇기와 뒤집기를 통해 성립하는 독특한 '반어체'이다. 훼손되고 뒤틀린 것을 찾아 폭로하되, 그러나 어떤 절대적 준거로써 재단하는 단호한 자신만만함은 없기에 그 반어체는 풍자적이지 않고 오히려 비애 서린 해학에 더 가까운 분위기를 지닌다.　　　　　김윤식

Su Jung-in exposes the disconnect between those notions that rule our consciousness and reality, and the distortion by this reality. This is why his fictions abound with fun and whimsy from wordplay, while their subtlety demands a careful reading. Su's relativism and the supporting self-reflection give birth to a unique style of writing, namely, a conversational style and the unique "style of irony" established by simultaneous continuation and subversion of each sentence, bestowing new meanings to same words. Because it captures and exposes the damaged and the twisted, yet lacks the decisive confidence to judge them by absolute

그의 작품은 단편소설에 관한 한 우리 문학이 도달한 가장 높은 경지를 구현하고 있다고 할 수 있다. 그의 어느 작품을 펼쳐보더라도 우리는 꽉 짜인 구성과 치밀한 복선의 배치, 생동감 넘치는 대화, 경제적인 언어 구사를 통한 인물 성격의 부각, 적절한 반전에 의한 산뜻한 마무리 등 단편소설이 요구하는 미학적 황금률을 두루 충족시켜주고 있음을 발견하게 된다. 훌륭한 목수가 어떤 재질의 나무라도 능숙하게 깎고 다듬어 적재적소에 사용할 줄 알듯이 그는 어떤 소재라도 일정한 가공을 거쳐 독자의 의표를 찌르는 한 편의 소설로 완성시켜내는 역량을 지닌 작가이다.

남진우

끊임없이 기존의 소설 스타일을 넘어서서 새로운 소설 스타일을 탐색해온 서정인의 서사적 혁신 도정은 한마디로 소설을 소설답게 하는 소설성의 탐색이었으며, 그것은 또한 우리 삶에서 소설이란 무엇인가 하는 근본 질문에 답하려는 모색의 과정이었다고 할 수 있다. 물론 많은 작가들이 소설을 쓰면서 이런 질문과 탐색을 행하는 것이 사실이지만, 서정인만큼 소설 혹은 소설성

standards, this style of irony does not strike one as being sarcastic but comes closer to having an atmosphere of pathos-ridden humor.

Kim Yun-sik

Su Jung-in's works are at the zenith of contemporary Korean short fiction. We open any of his works to find that it satisfies the aesthetic golden rules demanded of a short fiction, such as a well-woven construction and the meticulous placement of a subplot, vivid dialogues, the accentuation of characters' personalities through economical use of language, and a clean-cut ending by way of a fitting plot twist. Just as an expert carpenter knows how to cut and shape any kind of wood skillfully and use it for precisely the right purpose, Su as an author has the capacity to take any subject, process it, and turn it into a completed work of fiction that catches the reader by surprise.

Nam Jin-u

The course of narrative innovation of Su Jung-in, who has searched ceaselessly for a new style of fiction beyond extant styles, has been, in short, a search for a fictionality that makes a fiction a fic-

그 자체에 대한 자의식을 특징적으로 드러내 보인 작가는 드문 편이다. 기존의 소설 스타일은 물론 자신의 과거 소설 스타일을 손쉽게 모사하여 재생산하는 소설적 매너리즘을 그는 기질적으로 거부한다.

우찬제

tion, as well as a process of exploring the fundamental question of what fiction means in our lives. While it is true, of course, that many authors have undertaken this inquiry and search while writing fiction, rarely has an author displayed the self-awareness of fiction or fictionality itself as specifically as Su. It is in his nature to resist the reproductive mannerism of fiction by easily imitating not only existing styles of fiction, but also his own style of fiction-writing from early periods.

U Chan-je

서정인

서정인은 1936년 12월 20일 전남 순천군 순천읍 장천리 253번지에서 아버지 서병량과 어머니 김영자의 차남으로 태어났다. 본명은 정택이다. 순천남소학교, 순천중학교, 순천고등학교를 졸업하고 1955년 서울대 문리대 영문학과에 입학하였다. 1962년 서울대 대학원 영문학과에 진학하였으며, 12월에 단편「후송」이《사상계》신인상에 뽑혀 등단하였다. 1964년 대학원을 졸업한 후, 1968년 10월 전북대학교 문리과대학 영문학과에 전임강사로 부임하였다. 이후 1989년에 인문과학대학 학장에 취임하였고, 2002년 봄에 정년퇴임 하였다. 서정인은 여러 차례의 외국 체험을 통해 문학적인 폭과 넓이를 지속적으로 확장시킨 작가이다. 1971년부터 1973년까지 미국 하버드 연경학원 연구원으로 유학하였으며, 이때 철학자인 박이문과 교류하였다. 1977년 여름에는 풀브라이트 재단 후원으로 미국 털사대학에 가서 3년간 유학하였다. 1996년 회갑을 맞이하였을 때는 방문 연구원으로 옥스퍼드를 방문하였다. 서정인은 이청

Su Jung-in

Su Jung-in was born on December 20th, 1936, at 253 Jangcheon-ri, Suncheon-eup, Suncheon-gun, Jeollanam-do, as the younger son of Su Byeong-ryang and Kim Yeong-ja. His real name is Jung-taek. After graduating from South Suncheon Elementary School, Suncheon Middle School and Suncheon High School, he enrolled in the English Department of the College of Humanities at Seoul National University in 1955. He began a graduate program in the same department at the same school in 1962; in December of that year, he made his literary debut when he won *Sasanggye*'s new writer prize with his short story, "Evacuation." After finishing the graduate school with a Master's degree in 1964, he was appointed a full-time lecturer in the English Literature department in the College of Humanities at Chonbuk National University in October 1968. He became Dean of the College of Arts and Sciences at the University in 1989, and retired in the spring of 2002.

Su Jung-in is a writer who has continuously ex-

준, 김승옥 등과 더불어 1960년대를 대표하는 작가로서 인정받고 있다. 그의 작품들은 문학적 간접화의 방법을 통해 사건의 진상에 다가가는 양상을 보여준다. 특히 현대인이 노정하게 마련인 자의식의 분열을 추적하는 지식인 소설의 면모를 보이기도 한다. 등단한 이래 50여 년 동안 꾸준한 작품 활동을 통해 새로운 소설 기법을 추구해온 작가의 작품 세계는 경박한 이 시대에 사유의 깊이를 느끼게 해주는 뛰어난 문학적 성과를 거둔 것으로 평가된다. 이러한 그의 문학적 성취에 걸맞게 서정인은 수많은 문학상을 수상하였다. 1976년 한국문학사 제정 한국문학작가상, 1983년 월탄문학상, 1986년 한국일보사 제정 한국문학창작상, 1995년 동서문학상, 1999년 제1회 동리문학상과 제7회 대산문학상, 2002년 이산문학상을 수상하였다.

panded his literary breadth and depth with his numerous experiences abroad. He was a researcher at Harvard University's Yenching Institute from 1971 to 1973, during which time he interacted with the philosopher Park Yi-mun. In 1977, he went to study at the University of Tulsa for three years on a Fulbright scholarship. He celebrated his sixtieth birthday in 1996 at Oxford as a visiting scholar.

Su Jung-in is widely acknowledged as a writer representing the 1960s along with such authors as Yi Cheong-jun and Kim Seung-ok. His works exhibit an approach to the truth of the matter via literary indirection. Specifically, they also show an aspect of the intellectual fiction by pursuing the division of self-consciousness prevalent in the present era. The literary domain of Su, who has sought new styles of fiction by writing consistently for the past 50 years since his literary debut, has been recognized for its outstanding literary achievement of allowing the reader to feel the profundity of thought in this age of frivolity.

Su Jung-in has won numerous literary awards for his literary accomplishment. He won the Korean Literary Author Award given by Hanguk Munhak-sa in 1976, the Woltan Literary Award in 1983, the Korean Creative Literary Award given by *Hankook Ilbo*-sa in 1986, the Dongsuh(East-West) Literary Award in 1995, the inaugural Dongri Literary Award and the seventh annual Daesan Literary Award, both in 1999, and the Yi Sang Literary Award in 2002.

번역 **제이미 챙** Translated by Jamie Chang

김애란 단편집 『침이 고인다』 번역으로 한국문학번역원 번역지원금을 받아 번역 활동을 시작했다. 구병모 장편소설 『위저드 베이커리』 번역으로 코리아 타임즈 현대문학번역 장려상을 수상했다.

Jamie Chang has translated Kim Ae-ran's *Mouthwatering* and Koo Byung-mo's *The Wizard Bakery* on KLTI translation grants, and received the Modern Korean Literature Translation Commendation Prize in 2010. She received her master's degree in Regional Studies□East Asia from Harvard in 2011.

감수 **전승희, 데이비드 윌리엄 홍**
Edited by Jeon Seung-hee and David William Hong

전승희는 서울대학교와 하버드대학교에서 영문학과 비교문학으로 박사 학위를 받았으며, 현재 하버드대학교 한국학 연구소의 연구원으로 재직하며 아시아 문예 계간지 《ASIA》 편집위원으로 활동 중이다. 현대 한국문학 및 세계문학을 다룬 논문을 다수 발표했으며, 바흐친의 『장편소설과 민중언어』, 제인 오스틴의 『오만과 편견』 등을 공역했다. 1988년 한국여성연구소의 창립과 《여성과 사회》의 창간에 참여했고, 2002년부터 보스턴 지역 피학대 여성을 위한 단체인 '트랜지션하우스' 운영에 참여해 왔다. 2006년 하버드대학교 한국학 연구소에서 '한국 현대사와 기억'을 주제로 한 워크숍을 주관했다.

Jeon Seung-hee is a member of the Editorial Board of *ASIA*, is a Fellow at the Korea Institute, Harvard University. She received a Ph.D. in English Literature from Seoul National University and a Ph.D. in Comparative Literature from Harvard University. She has presented and published numerous papers on modern Korean and world literature. She is also a co-translator of Mikhail Bakhtin's *Novel and the People's Culture* and Jane Austen's *Pride and Prejudice*. She is a founding member of the Korean Women's Studies Institute and of the biannual Women's Studies' journal *Women and Society* (1988), and she has been working at 'Transition House,' the first and oldest shelter for battered women in New England. She organized a workshop entitled "The Politics of Memory in Modern Korea" at the Korea Institute, Harvard University, in 2006. She also served as an advising committee member for the Asia-Africa Literature Festival in 2007 and for the POSCO Asian Literature Forum in 2008.

데이비드 윌리엄 홍은 미국 일리노이주 시카고에서 태어났다. 일리노이대학교에서 영문학을, 뉴욕대학교에서 영어교육을 공부했다. 지난 2년간 서울에 거주하면서 처음으로 한국인과 아시아계 미국인 문학에 깊이 몰두할 기회를 가졌다. 현재 뉴욕에서 거주하며 강의와 저술 활동을 한다.

David William Hong was born in 1986 in Chicago, Illinois. He studied English Literature at the University of Illinois and English Education at New York University. For the past two years, he lived in Seoul, South Korea, where he was able to immerse himself in Korean and Asian-American literature for the first time. Currently, he lives in New York City, teaching and writing.

바이링궐 에디션 한국 대표 소설 036
무자년의 가을 사흘

2013년 11월 14일 초판 1쇄 인쇄 | 2013년 11월 21일 초판 1쇄 발행

지은이 서정인 | 옮긴이 제이미 챙 | 펴낸이 방재석
감수 전승희, 데이비드 윌리엄 홍 | 기획 정은경, 전성태, 이경재
편집 정수인, 이은혜 | 관리 박신영 | 디자인 이춘희
펴낸곳 아시아 | 출판등록 2006년 1월 31일 제319-2006-4호
주소 서울특별시 동작구 흑석동 100-16
전화 02.821.5055 | 팩스 02.821.5057 | 홈페이지 www.bookasia.org
ISBN 978-89-94006-94-9 (set) | 978-89-94006-18-5 (04810)
값은 뒤표지에 있습니다.

Bi-lingual Edition Modern Korean Literature 036
Three Days of Autumn, 1948

Written by Su Jung-in | Translated by Jamie Chang
Published by Asia Publishers | 100-16 Heukseok-dong, Dongjak-gu, Seoul, Korea
Homepage Address www.bookasia.org | Tel. (822).821.5055 | Fax. (822).821.5057
First published in Korea by Asia Publishers 2013
ISBN 978-89-94006-94-9 (set) | 978-89-94006-18-5 (04810)